By the time William's bulky form stood in the entrance of the closet, I was human and 100 percent naked, though I didn't have time to worry about it. There was a creep out there after my manly man.

"Not real quick with the nonverbals, are you?" I propped my hands on my hips.

He copied the gesture. I had to admit, his version was much more intimidating. And not just because he was actually wearing clothes. "You want to tell me what that was all about?"

"Look, a couple of freaks are looking for you. They had your picture and everything."

"What?"

"Yeah, these guys—who gave me chills, by the way—stopped into the café and wanted to know if we'd seen you. They were evil. I mean, to the core. And they definitely weren't from around here."

He reached out and gripped my shoulder. "What did they look like?"

"Like a couple of thugs in an amateur production of Oklahoma."

At his blank look, I gave him a more specific description. "So, Mafia Hit Man is out there right now, looking for you. And you stood there, a hulking target, just begging to be caught."

"Sorry, I don't speak coyote."

Welcome to

Dreamspun Beyond

Dear Reader,

Everyone knows love brings a touch of magic to your life. And the presence of paranormal thrills can make a romance that much more exciting. Dreamspun Beyond selections tell stories of love featuring your favorite shifters, vampires, wizards, and more falling in love amid paranormal twists. Stories that make your breath catch and your imagination soar.

In the pages of these imaginative love stories, readers can escape to a contemporary world flavored with a touch of the paranormal where love conquers all despite challenges, the thrill of a first kiss sweeps you away, and your heart pounds at the sight of the one you love. When you put it all together, you discover romance in its truest form, no matter what world you come from.

Love sees no difference.

Elizabeth North

Executive Director
Dreamspinner Press

j. leigh bailey

STALKING BUFFALO BILL

PUBLISHED BY

DREAMSPINNER
PRESS

Published by
DREAMSPINNER PRESS

5032 Capital Circle SW, Suite 2, PMB# 279,
Tallahassee, FL 32305-7886 USA
www.dreamspinnerpress.com

This is a work of fiction. Names, characters, places, and incidents either
are the product of author imagination or are used fictitiously, and any
resemblance to actual persons, living or dead, business establishments,
events, or locales is entirely coincidental.

Stalking Buffalo Bill
© 2017 j. leigh bailey.

Cover Art
© 2017 Aaron Anderson.
aaronbydesign55@gmail.com
Cover content is for illustrative purposes only and any person depicted
on the cover is a model.

ISBN: 978-1-63533-753-2
Digital ISBN: 978-1-63533-754-9
Library of Congress Control Number: 2017904706
Published September 2017
v. 1.0

Printed in the United States of America
∞
This paper meets the requirements of
ANSI/NISO Z39.48-1992 (Permanence of Paper).

J. LEIGH BAILEY is an office drone by day and romance author by night. She can usually be found with her nose in a book or pressed up against her computer monitor. A book-a-day reading habit sometimes gets in the way of… well, everything… but some habits aren't worth breaking. She's been reading romance novels since she was ten years old. The last twenty years or so have not changed her voracious appetite for stories of romance, relationships, and achieving that vitally important Happily Ever After. She's a firm believer that everyone, no matter their gender, age, sexual orientation, or paranormal affiliation, deserves a happy ending.

She wrote her first story at seven which was, unbeknownst to her at the time, a charming piece of fan fiction in which Superman battled (and defeated, of course) the nefarious X Luther. (She was quite put out to be told later that the character's name was supposed to be Lex.) Her second masterpiece should have been a bestseller, but the action-packed tale of rescuing her little brother from an alligator attack in the marshes of Florida collected dust for years under the bed instead of gaining critical acclaim.

Now she writes about boys traversing the crazy world of love, relationships, and acceptance. Find out more at www.jleighbailey.net or email her at j.leigh.bailey@gmail.com.

Thank you to Team Donnie—my critique partners and the supportive members of Windy City RWA, especially Stephanie, Kelly, Kristen, and Ann Marie. Your support and enthusiasm for this project kept me motivated throughout.

Chapter One

"YOU know stalking's a crime, right?"

I jerked away from the glass display case I'd been leaning on and glared at my friend Ford. "It's not stalking. I don't follow him around or anything. *He* comes *here*." I swiped a towel across the gleaming surface of the pastry case. It didn't need it, but just in case a little drool slipped out of my mouth. "It's staring."

Ford filled the espresso machine's hopper with fragrant coffee beans. "It's ridiculous, is what it is."

He would never understand. "But he's just so… so… so *manly*."

Ford snorted. "As opposed to what, girly?"

It didn't matter what Ford said. The manly man I spent hours every day ogling, and several more hours a day daydreaming about, was worth every stalkerish second. For the last eight months, he'd come into Buddy's Café every day, sat at the same small table by the fireplace, and read a book or a magazine or fiddled on his tablet computer. He really was a masculine work of art. Tall and broad as a mountain, and I wanted nothing more than to climb him. Dark curly hair, a thick beard. Not one of those unkempt, No-Shave-November deals. It was neatly trimmed, but long enough I wanted to tangle my fingers in it.

"Donnie, you're staring again."

Damn it. I dragged my eyes away. I couldn't help it, though. Today my manly man wore an oatmeal-colored sweater that should have looked bland but instead looked soft and cozy. My inner coyote pup wanted to snuggle into the plush knit and soak up his heat.

"And you have customers." Ford nudged me, and I had to once again forcibly draw my eyes away from the man.

I tucked one end of the towel into the back pocket of my jeans and helped customers. Luckily I could practically do this job in my sleep since my mind stayed focused on my manly man instead of taking coffee and muffin orders. Things I knew about my little— er, big—obsession: his name was William, he liked his coffee black, his pastries savory instead of sweet, and whatever he did for a living gave him a couple of hours a day to hang out in a cozy coffee shop in Cody, Wyoming. Oh, and he was a shifter, but for the life of me, I couldn't figure out what kind.

There were a lot of shifters in this part of Wyoming, partly due to Cody's proximity to Yellowstone. But the town was also home to one of the only available shifter-friendly colleges this side of the Mississippi. Local humans didn't know it, but a bunch of the students at Cody College were shifters of one kind or another. There weren't a lot of places where animal shifters could attend school and have access to miles of forests, lakes, and mountains, and where classes could be modified to fit the special needs of the occasionally furry.

As a part-time coyote, my sense of smell was particularly keen. Which meant I immediately picked up the rich scents of musk and something herby, like sagebrush and grass. And, like his cozy sweater, the smell made me want to roll all over him.

I glanced at the clock above the stone fireplace in the corner. It was time. If I waited any longer, he'd get up and leave. "I'm taking my break." I untied my forest-green apron and tossed it on the counter by the register.

Ford scowled at me. "It's almost eleven. We have to prep for the lunch crowd."

"I won't be long." I rushed to the back room.

The back room was about the size of a coat closet and held a small desk with a computer monitor, a safe, and a folding chair. There wasn't space for anything else. I reached under the desk and grabbed the insulated bag I'd brought with me this morning. I pulled out the rectangular storage container, inhaling the distinctive basil-and-parmesan scent. My stomach lurched. It wasn't the scones—they smelled fantastic—it was nerves. I'd been planning this moment for weeks. Now the time had finally come, and it struck me as stupid, potentially humiliating, and maybe a little dangerous. After all, what did I really know about my manly man?

"Don't wuss out now," I ordered myself, gripping the plastic box.

Before I could second-guess myself again, I pushed out of the back room and strode to the dining area with as much swagger as I could manage. Coyotes were good at bluffing, especially among the bigger predators.

William looked up from his newspaper. Jesus, those deep brown eyes should be outlawed. How was a guy supposed to remember anything while drowning in those coffee-colored irises?

He cleared his throat.

After an embarrassingly long pause—yeah, words really weren't happening for me at that moment—he arched a brow. "Did you need something?"

"*Scones.*" I cringed. I'd blurted the word out a little too loudly.

He cocked his head. "Scones?" His voice was deep and rumbly, and I quivered at the sound.

I nodded. "Exactly. Scones."

"What about them?"

I cleared my throat. From the corner of my eye, I saw Ford smirking at me. Damn, I seriously needed to get my shit together. "I made some. I wondered if you wanted any?"

He glanced down at his plate, which held half of an onion bagel with cream cheese. "I'm fine."

I sucked in a breath. Whatever I'd hoped to accomplish with this little interaction was going to explode in my face if I didn't get my head out of my ass. "No, I know. I mean, I'm trying a new recipe, and I hoped you'd taste test it for me." I shoved the box toward him. "I noticed you stay away from our sweeter items, but you like the more savory bagels and such. And, well, I came up with a sun-dried tomato, basil, and parmesan scone recipe I thought you might like."

He leaned back in his chair, the move showcasing the amazing breadth of his chest. "You didn't have anyone else who could test them for you?" He was so hard to read. He didn't seem opposed to the idea. Not standoffish. Reserved, maybe? Like he wasn't used to people approaching him with savory treats.

"Well, my friend Ford," I said, bobbing my head toward the front counter, "is allergic to tomatoes. And my family tends to be a bit boring in their tastes. Real red-meat-and-potatoes kind of people. They think they're being exotic when they eat bison instead of beef."

William's mouth pressed into a thin line, and for a second I thought I'd made him mad. Maybe it was the meat comment? "Are you a vegetarian? I know some people don't even want to talk about meat and food in the same sentence. Too gory for them, maybe." On the edge of babbling, I snapped my jaw closed.

"It's fine," William said after a minute. "I'm a vegetarian, but I'm not squeamish." He took the container from me. "Thanks. I'll let you know."

I shifted from foot to foot. *C'mon, Donnie. Say something.* Seriously, I was usually better than this. I've asked dudes out before. Even dudes I wasn't sure were gay. I hoped it wasn't wishful thinking, but I kind of suspected William was of the man-loving persuasion. Sometimes, from the corner of my eye, I was positive I'd caught him watching me. And not in the absent way so many people eyed servers and clerks. No, I'd catch in him a predatory heat that didn't quite match his studious solitude. That, in addition to my own little crush, was what prompted me to attempt my scone-based seduction. So really, there was no reason for this to be so awkward.

"Is there something else?" He watched me from under thick, straight brows.

I guessed he was older than me by a decade, but I refused to let the possible age gap or intimidating stare put me off. Especially since it kind of turned me on.

"Oh, and I'm Donnie. Donnie Granger?" Shit. Now I sounded like an adolescent girl, all questions and enthusiasm.

His gaze flicked to my nametag, eyes crinkling, and it looked like he tried not to smile. "William," he said.

"Oh, I know." Again, I sounded a bit too enthusiastic. I licked my lips, racking my brain for something to say, anything to keep the conversation going. And preferably in a way that wouldn't make me sound like a junior-high schooler. "What do you do?"

"About what?" William pushed his newspaper aside, and I took the gesture as an invitation. If he'd wanted me to go away, he'd have tried to read it, right?

"You know," I said, dropping into the chair across from his at the small table. "For a living. A job. For fun. Whatever. You're here almost every morning. It's made me curious." Crap. That made me sound like a stalker, didn't it? No, not a stalker. An observant customer-service person. Right.

He pushed back from the table far enough he could cross one leg over the other, and his grassy, sagey scent wafted toward me. It was all I could do to stop my tongue from lolling out of my mouth like a dog. "I'm a professor of history and politics over at CC." He paused. "The special track."

Ah, that meant he taught some of the shifter-only classes.

"Damn, if I'd had a professor like you, I probably wouldn't have dropped out."

He raised his brows.

Double crap. If I wanted to impress a professor, mentioning I was a college dropout probably wasn't the best way. "How long have you been teaching there?" I kept myself—barely—from adding that I hadn't seen him around before February. And believe me, if he'd been anywhere near town before that, I'd have noticed. Even if his looks didn't trip every one of my personal triggers, there was no way I'd miss his scent. But he didn't need to know how obsessively I tracked him.

"Started with the spring semester."

"Cool." Jesus, I was a moron. *Cool?* Maybe I needed to go back to school after all. Conversation 101 was looking more and more necessary. Then, after that, I could attend Flirting for Dummies.

"What about you?" he asked, thankfully not put off by my abysmal interpersonal communication skills.

"Me?"

"Yes, what do you do?"

"Oh, right." I pushed my chair back so it balanced on its rear legs. "Well, I work here, obviously. I'm taking a photography class at the community center. I spend a lot of time riding herd on my dozen or so nieces and nephews. I bake a lot." Realizing I sounded like a college application, or worse, an online dating profile, I produced my toothiest cheesy grin. "And I like long walks on the beach at sunset."

William's lips twitched.

"Hey, Donnie!"

I growled low in my throat. The place better be under armed attack or I was going to strangle Ford. Didn't he see I was finally making progress with my manly man? I turned my head to glare at my soon-to-be-ex-best friend. He glared right back, jerking his head to indicate the long line at the register.

"Damn." I let the chair drop back into place, then stood. "I'd better get back to work. Let me know how you like the scones," I said over my shoulder as I headed back to the front counter.

He nodded. "I will. And thanks for thinking of me." He tapped the container of pastries.

"No problem. Hope you like them."

A few minutes later, while I was elbow-deep in lattes and danishes, William left the café. When he opened the door, the wind blew in, carrying with it the aroma of fall leaves and sagebrush.

THREE hours and a bazillion customers later—okay, maybe I exaggerated—Buddy's was finally mostly empty again. A couple of college students huddled over laptops in one corner, but that was it.

"You're wasting your time, you know." Ford. King of the non sequitur.

"Huh?" I wasn't going to give him the satisfaction of knowing my mind was exactly where he suspected it was. Wow, even to myself, my thought processes were convoluted.

Ford was my best friend and roommate. We'd met during my first year at college. Somebody had thought it was a good idea to place a hyperactive, easily distractible coyote shifter with an intense, perpetually grumpy bird of prey. *Somebody*, apparently, knew what they were doing. We'd been roommates ever since. Even though I'd dropped out of school after two years of hopping from one major to another, and Ford was now a graduate student in the biology department, we still managed to make things work. But this meant Ford knew me a little too well.

He rolled his eyes. "The big guy. I don't see you as his type."

I propped my fists on my hips, hopefully hiding the sudden insecurity. "Hey, you're my best friend. You're supposed to be on my side."

"I am on your side. But when he breaks your heart by his complete lack of interest, I'm the one who'll have to deal with your moping around for days."

"I don't mope."

He narrowed his golden amber eyes. "You're a champion moper. Remember Tony?"

"Tony doesn't count. He totally led me on. He flirted with me, even tried to talk me into bed, and the bastard was married. No way was that my fault."

"And Jack?"

"Okay, well, Jack was kind of my fault."

"You get so obsessed, and you refuse to see them for who they are. Then you're shocked when they turn out to be assholes."

I slumped against the counter. I sometimes wished my best friend didn't know me so well.

"Besides," Ford added as he dug into a low cupboard for a sleeve of to-go cups, "there's something shady about the guy."

I straightened from my slouch. "What do you mean? There's nothing shady about him."

Ford snorted. "He hangs out here almost every day. He doesn't talk to anyone. He always orders the same thing."

"Large coffee, black." I nodded.

"He comes in at the same time."

"Ten a.m."

"And he leaves at noon."

I shook my head. "How does any of this make him shady? So he's a creature of habit. That's not a bad thing. You follow the same schedule nearly every day too."

"Yeah, it's called a work and school schedule. I wouldn't be here every day like clockwork if I didn't have to. Jesus, Donnie, if that's not suspicious, then he's got to be the most boring man in the world."

"Boring isn't bad." I had a terrible need to defend William, even though we barely knew each other. Maybe because I wanted so badly to know him better.

"Boring would drive you crazy within moments."

Maybe. But that was only a problem if William truly was boring, which I seriously doubted. No one with that kind of intensity, contained though it was, could actually be boring.

"What the hell are they wearing?"

Even as Ford asked the question, the smell of gun oil and smog assaulted me. I followed the acrid scent and Ford's gaze to two tall men who tried so hard to fit in, they stood out. We'd seen it before when city people visited. For some reason there were people who thought Wyoming meant cowboy country. Okay, well, Wyoming *was* cowboy country, but these guys looked like they went to a fancy boutique to get the official high-end cowboy outfits.

Everything they wore was too new, too contrived. From the blade-edge creases in their designer jeans to the shimmer of silver on boot toes and the black hats on their heads, it was too much. Little things gave away that these weren't their usual outfits. For one, their hats. A man's relationship with his hat was a very personal one. You couldn't just plop a hat on your head and call it good. You had to adjust the brim and perfect the fit. It took weeks, sometimes months, to wear them right. Their hats sat awkwardly, a little high, and clearly hadn't been touched more than needed to drop them on the men's heads. Then there were the bolo ties. Seriously? Not even my dad wore one of those. My grandpa pulled his out for special dress-up occasions, but no one younger than him would be caught dead with a bolo tie.

Some people made the strangest assumptions about Wyoming. These guys apparently were trying to blend in. Well, they failed. Epically.

The two men stood stiff and straight near the bulletin board, like they were checking out offers for tutoring or interested in buying a 1987 Volvo. Their eyes weren't scanning the notices, though; they scanned every corner and booth in the café.

Talk about shady.

Part of me, the part running on instinct, wanted to chase them out of the café, but the other part of me wanted to know what they were doing here more. "Welcome to Buddy's," I said as one of the guys—this one a thirtysomething blond whose hair had started receding—looked in our direction.

The men shot glances at each other and held some kind of silent conversation over the next thirty seconds. Balding Blond Guy nodded in our direction and strode to the front counter. "Howdy."

I decided not to question the greeting. Some people around here said howdy, but not many. And this dude sounded as awkward as he looked in his pseudo-cowboy clothes.

"Hiya. Can I get you something?"

"Actually," the other guy, this one reminding me of a mafia hit man with his bulging muscles, shaved head, and aggression pouring off him in waves, said, "we're looking for someone. We've been told he hangs out here." He pulled a smartphone out of his pocket, swiped the screen, and turned the device in my direction.

I sucked in a breath, then tried really hard to still my face. The phone displayed an image of William. But not reserved college professor William who'd invaded my dreams and refused to leave. Instead the guy in the picture was hard, almost feral. He glared at someone outside the frame, lips pulled back in a snarl, eyes flashing dangerously. Intimidating as hell, but also sexy as fuck.

I motioned for the phone, and Mafia Hit Man passed it to me. I looked closer to make sure it wasn't someone else, someone who just happened to look like William. It was definitely him. Two main questions bloomed in my head. First, why were these two shady dudes looking for William? Second, what would it be like to be around William when he wasn't his normal reserved self?

I squinted and cocked my head, playing it up. "Sorry. I thought for a minute I might have seen him, but I was wrong." I turned the phone to face Ford. "You don't recognize him, do you?" I narrowed my eyes at him, silently ordering him to play along.

For once he did as I wanted. I probably needed to rethink the whole ex-best-friend thing from earlier. "Never seen him."

"Why do I think you're lying?"

In my furry form, my hackles would have risen from the cold menace in Mafia Hit Man's voice. "Maybe you should see a psychologist? I've heard suspicion and paranoia are signs of several mental disorders."

Balding Blond Guy narrowed his eyes. "What's that supposed to mean?"

I blinked at him, going for my most innocent, angelic expression. "Nothing."

He took a step forward, but Mafia Hit Man stopped him with a hand on his shoulder. "Are you sure? This man is very dangerous. It's important we find him before anyone gets hurt."

"Why? What did he do?"

I kicked Ford's ankle. What the hell was he doing?

The two strangers looked at each other, holding another silent conversation. Balding Blond Guy plastered a sincere but somber expression on his face. "I'm afraid we're not free to divulge that information at this time."

Now they were trying to make it sound like they were some kind of law enforcement agents. Clearly, these guys were not going to win any Oscars.

Mafia Hit Man reached behind his back, and I tensed. The bastard wasn't going to pull a gun on us, was he?

Instead he passed me a white business card with a name and phone number. Earl Palmer. Seriously? Earl? He totally looked like a Carmine. Oh well, he'd always be Mafia Hit Man to me.

"Please contact us immediately if you see this man."

I let the card drop to the counter. "Sure." See, they weren't the only ones who could lie.

The second the café door closed behind them, Ford spun toward me. "Holy shit. What the fuck was that?"

"Definitely shady."

"Do you think your professor dude really is dangerous?"

I shook my head. "He's a *professor*. And you yourself called him the world's most boring man. Doesn't strike me as dangerous." I craned my neck so I could see out the café's front window. "I'm going to find out what's going on."

"Why?"

"I'm worried about William. I need to warn him."

"Donnie." Ford released a long-suffering sigh. "Your reckless curiosity is going to come back and bite you in the ass someday."

I ignored him. Sometimes that was the only way to deal with Ford. I ducked into the small office, then

tugged off my clothes and tossed them at Ford, who'd
followed me. He rolled his eyes and started to fold my
jeans while I initiated the shift into my coyote form.
I'd seen movies and read books that made it seem like
changing to our alternate form was horribly painful,
with stretching muscles, cracking bones, and snapping
tendons. Thank God fiction is stranger than reality, even
for a secret paranormal race. My shift was easy. I just
had to picture the coyote's form in my head, and then
presto chango, I was a coyote. No pain, just a tiny pop
of tension releasing, kind of like a full-body sneeze.

I picked up the new-clothes scent of the men the
second I stepped around the counter. Then I sneezed
at their caustic smell. Urban decay. Smog. Garbage.
Piss. Blood. Some odors were so ingrained in a body,
no amount of scrubbing or soaking could erase them.
These guys had been surrounded by enough evil that
even their souls were scarred. I snorted to clear my
nose before shooting a quick look to the students in the
corner. I recognized both as fellow shifters, so it was
safe to cross the dining room. I jogged to the entrance
and pointed my snout in the direction of the door.

Grumbling under his breath, Ford crossed the room
and let me out. "I hope you know what you're doing."

I yipped in affirmation and let my nose lead me. I
was on a mission to save my manly man.

Chapter Two

THE normally clean Wyoming air assaulted me with the mingled scents of crisp autumn and urban violence. The fall temperature was cool, but the sun shone brightly in the sky. I slunk through the shadows as best I could, following the acrid stench. Halfway down the block, I caught sight of the starched plaid shirts standing at the corner, so I ducked into the nearest alley. The two guys looked like they were arguing. Mafia Hit Man jabbed his finger past Balding Blond Guy, pointing in the direction of Buddy's. I edged deeper into the shadows and crouched low.

I strained to hear over the grumble of diesel trucks. Unfortunately, good as my hearing is, I was too far away to make out much more than a word or two. I caught the name Conrad, the word *pissed*, and something about *the base* before Mafia Hit Man jogged across the street and Balding Blond Guy slid into the driver's seat of a black sedan with tinted windows. Apparently their attempts to blend in didn't include their vehicles.

They split up, which put me in the awkward position of deciding whom to follow. Finally I trotted after Mafia Hit Man since he headed in the direction of the college. Traffic along the street was stopped for a red light, so I took my chances and ran full-out. Hopefully if anyone saw me, they'd think I was a dog. Natural coyotes showed up in town every now and then, but I would be a lot safer if everyone assumed I was a weird mixed breed that only resembled a coyote. Shotgun pellets in the ass were nobody's idea of fun.

I breathed a little easier when I reached the campus. There were a handful of trees and bushes to provide cover, for one thing. For another, Cody College was known around here as Shifter U, so a large number of the students and staff were shifters who would recognize what I was and wouldn't call animal control. Getting caught by the humans was still a risk—avoiding discovery by humans was rule numero uno at Shifter U—but it was one I had to take.

A wave of something green and herby cut across my path, and I had to fight my coyote for control. He wanted to follow the scent we knew would lead to William. Human-me, on the other hand, understood we had a mission and couldn't afford to be distracted. It's a lot harder to fight instinct when I'm in coyote form. I may have had a human mind inside the coyote's body, but sometimes the primitive desires—like the desire for sex—overwhelmed human logic. I needed to move forward, to follow Mafia Hit Man, but I couldn't force my legs to take the necessary steps. Muscles tightened in my haunches, and I dug my paws into the grass. *He's getting away! Move, you mangy mutt!*

I snarled and finally pulled myself back on track. I'd never had a problem like that before. Never had to fight between my will and my instincts.

Mafia Hit Man's phone chimed, and he pulled it out of his pocket and stared. He paused on the sidewalk and tapped on the screen.

A burst of laughter from one of the buildings drew my attention. A group of students descended the steps, snarking about something their professor had said. I didn't pay attention to the details. William stood at the top of the stairs, digging into his shoulder bag. My gaze flew to Mafia Hit Man. If he looked up from his phone, William would be directly in his line of sight.

I didn't have time to stop and think. I charged toward William, yipping and growling to get his attention. I didn't want to draw Mafia Hit Man's notice, which meant I had to do it quietly. Urgently and quietly was not an easy combination. How did I get myself into these situations?

I hit the bottom step and leaped to the landing. Finally William looked up from his bag. He didn't step back in alarm, as I would have if a coyote charged me from out of nowhere. Instead he threw back his shoulders and lowered his head to spear me with a glower that had me scrambling to a halt at his feet.

I whimpered, internally cursing my inability to talk in this form. I snagged the leg of his khaki pants and tugged, urging him back toward the building. He didn't budge. I was trying to help him, damn it. The least he could do was cooperate. I took a couple of steps back and glared.

He raised an eyebrow at me. His face softened a bit, so he must have recognized me. So whatever his shift was, the animal had good sense of smell since William had never seen me in shifted form. He still didn't move, though. I yipped again and bit down on William's pant leg.

"If you tear my pants, I'm going to be pissed." He said it so calmly I wanted to strangle him. Did he think I was playing?

I glanced down the lawn. Mafia Hit Man was talking to a student who pointed to the social sciences building. We were out of time.

Screw it. I released his pants and snarled at him, then hopped and grabbed his bag's strap between my teeth and pulled it off his shoulder. The minute it landed on the step, I ran into the building, dragging his bag behind me.

He cursed and strode after me, his long legs allowing him to keep me in sight.

A custodian pushed a cleaning cart out of a closet to my right. Before the door closed behind him, I darted into the small room. The old man—who smelled a lot like a beaver—harrumphed but didn't do or say anything else. Clearly he was used to odd happenings at Shifter U.

I dropped the strap of William's satchel and stood back so I had room to shift.

By the time William's bulky form stood in the entrance of the closet, I was human and 100 percent naked, though I didn't have time to worry about it. There was a creep out there after my manly man.

"Not real quick with the nonverbals, are you?" I propped my hands on my hips.

He copied the gesture. I had to admit, his version was much more intimidating. And not just because he was actually wearing clothes. "You want to tell me what that was all about?"

I rolled my eyes. "Obviously I needed to get you alone."

His eyes trailed down my body, from the top of my sandy-brown hair to the tips of my toes. Heat prickled along every inch his eyes touched. Flustered, I snapped, "Not for that."

"Too bad."

Did he really—no, now wasn't the time for that.

"Look, a couple of freaks are looking for you. They had your picture and everything."

The slight smirk he wore slipped off his face. "What?"

"Yeah, these guys—who gave me chills, by the way—stopped by the café and wanted to know if we'd seen you. They were evil. I mean, to the core. And they definitely weren't from around here."

He reached out and gripped my shoulder. "What did they look like?"

"Like a couple of thugs in an amateur production of *Oklahoma*."

At his blank look, I gave him a more specific description of the weirdos. Then I told him what I'd seen. "So, Mafia Hit Man is out there right now, looking for you. And you stood there, a hulking target, just begging to be caught."

"Sorry, I don't speak coyote."

He wasn't really sorry. I could tell.

"So what are we going to do?" Now that the adrenaline had started to fade, I needed to focus on anything other than the fact that I was naked. In front of the man of my dreams. Alone. It was an even split on whether I was feeling more awkward or horny. Given the situation, horny seemed inappropriate, so I searched the shelves for something to cover myself with.

"We? This doesn't have anything to do with you."

"Excuse me? I just raced through town to save your ass. Of course it concerns me." I pulled out a supersized garbage bag. It might have worked, except the plastic was clear. I tossed it aside, then continued my search.

"I appreciate the warning," he said, "but you need to stay out of this."

I squatted to sort through some boxes in the corner.

"What are you looking for?" He sounded exasperated. Good.

"I need to cover my junk if we're going to have this conversation." I glanced over my shoulder to see him. "I can't exactly be caught running around campus naked, can I? I did that once, and it didn't turn out well. Too much tequila at a full-moon party. Never a good idea."

Grumbling under his breath, William pulled off the oatmeal-colored sweater I'd fantasized about earlier. He had a white T-shirt on underneath. He threw the sweater at me. I caught it, clutching the soft wool to my chest. It was still warm from his body heat, and I had to forcibly restrain myself from breathing in his scent from the material.

"Well?" He stared at me.

"What?" Despite my intentions, I inhaled and let the aroma of green grass, sagebrush, and herbs flood me.

"Put it on. We can't spend all day in the closet."

I snickered. "I never did like closets. I came out of mine years ago."

He shook his head, then cracked open the door to peek out. Clearly he wasn't amused at my little joke. I shrugged into the sweater, and the hem fell to my knees. Damn, he was big. Was he a bear shifter, maybe? That could account for the size. Not that there was always a direct correlation between human size and shifter size. Take me, for example. I'm pretty average-sized for a man—a couple of inches under six feet—but I shift into a forty-five-pound coyote. Still, I couldn't picture him as a ferret or anything small like that.

"I think we're clear." William pushed the door open, then took two steps out. The acrid scent of Mafia Hit Man crashed into me, followed by the sound of a door slamming.

"Shit, it's him." I grabbed William's arm and tugged him back into the custodian's closet. I'm not sure what I would have done if he hadn't cooperated; no way could I move him if he didn't want to be moved. I pulled the door shut behind us, then shut the light off in the little room, just in case it glowed through the gap under the door.

"Are you sure it's him?"

I stared at him. "Believe me, there's no mistaking the stench."

His nose wrinkled. "Yeah, it's distinctive, all right." He leaned his head against the door, as though trying to hear through it.

I didn't need to press against the door to know that Mafia Hit Man was making his way down the corridor, opening doors to check rooms. It was only a matter of time before he reached our end of the hall.

A door slammed. It couldn't be more than a few rooms away. Mafia Hit Man was close.

If we left, we'd get caught. If we didn't leave, we'd get caught. Those didn't seem like very good options. I scanned the closet, looking for inspiration.

William crossed his arms over his massive chest, and inspiration struck. I was going to get a chance to climb him like a mountain after all.

"Take off your shirt," I demanded, even as I pulled the borrowed sweater off and shoved it onto a half-empty wire rack in the corner.

"Excuse me?" He stood straighter, chest puffed out indignantly.

Another slam, this one really close.

"You heard me." I was too anxious, in too much of a hurry to wait for him to follow directions. I reached for the hem of the T-shirt and started tugging it free from the waistband of his pants.

"What the hell are you doing?"

"Camouflage." I urged him against the rack. Thankfully he was too confused to put up much of a fight.

Catching on, he took over the removal of his shirt, leaving my hands free to tackle his belt. He sucked in a breath as my fingers slipped between cotton and hot skin. Man, what I wouldn't give to be doing this for real, somewhere I could take my time and enjoy revealing every inch of him.

The nasty smell of Mafia Hit Man came closer, ruining the moment for me.

I leaped at William, looped my arms around his neck, and wrapped my legs around his waist. His hands landed automatically on my ass, which was perfect. What we were supposedly doing needed to be obvious. I worked one of my feet into his back pocket and pushed his pants down as far as my leg would reach. Just as the doorknob turned, I dragged William's head to my chest. With my back to the door, no one would be able to identify William.

Two things hit me the second the door was wrenched open. First, Mafia Hit Man had seen my face, so I had to somehow keep him from recognizing me. And second, William wasn't wearing underwear.

"Dude! Get out. Can't you see we're busy?" I growled, trying to keep my head angled away from the light. I rocked against William, putting on a show. Only problem was both William and I were naked, and stressful situation or not, our bodies appreciated the friction. I sucked in a breath as my prick began to swell. Inappropriate? Absolutely. Could I stop it? Not even.

Mafia Hit Man grumbled something crude under his breath and slammed the door shut.

WE stayed like that for a long minute. William was probably listening to make sure Mafia Hit Man had cleared out. Me, well, I didn't have enough willpower to actually separate our bodies. All that hot flesh and thick muscle pressed against mine. The hair covering his chest tickled and sensitized my skin, and I squirmed, increasing the sensation. William gasped.

I buried my fingers in the thick waves of his hair and tilted his head back so I could see his face. "Would I be completely out of line if I kissed you? I've kind of been obsessing about it for a while now. I know the timing isn't great, but, you know, when the opportunity strikes—"

He lunged forward, stopping my words with the possessive press of his lips against mine. It was hot, hungry, and everything I could have dreamed of. His hands clutched my ass, pushing me farther up his body. My muscles had apparently dissolved, so I'd have fallen to a puddle at his feet if he hadn't supported my weight. And that he held my weight so easily, without any obvious strain, was sexy as fuck. Shifters were strong, but I wasn't exactly little.

Using teeth and tongue, he pried my mouth open, deepening the kiss with a fierceness and ferocity I hadn't expected. For such a quiet guy, he kissed like a beast. He claimed me, took me over completely, and I didn't mind at all.

I lost track of everything except his touch, his smell, so when the door opened again, it took a second to register. I hadn't heard or smelled anyone approaching. Which was a very bad sign. Balding Blond Guy and Mafia Hit Man were still out there looking for William. Most shifters might have supernatural senses, but they didn't do any good if we didn't pay attention to them.

The custodian—definitely a beaver—stood in the open doorway, hands propped on his hips. "Jay-sus, do you have to do that here? I don't go to your office when I get a piece of ass, do I?" He blinked when he got a good look at William. "Damn. I didn't expect to see you, Dr. Bryce."

William grunted and released his hold on me. I slid down his body to stand on my own shaking legs.

"Give us a minute, Mickey," William said, clearing his throat.

"Whatever you say." Mickey shook his head and turned away from the closet.

"That's going to be awkward." I nodded to where Mickey had been standing.

William hitched his pants back into place, then fastened the belt. A little thrill shot through me when I saw he was still partially erect. Although, come to think of it, the interruption hadn't done much to diminish my own stiffy. The musky scent of lust in the small space didn't do anything to help the situation. I caught the sweater William tossed at me, then slipped it back on.

William pulled on his T-shirt. "We need to talk."

"Yeah," I agreed. "Probably a good idea."

This time when we stepped out of the custodian's closet, there was so sign of Mafia Hit Man, and we made the hike to the second floor and William's office without running into anyone else. Which was a good thing, since I was wandering around in nothing but William's sweater.

When we reached his office, he pointed to an empty chair across from a desk buried under books and files. "Have a seat. I'll be right back."

"Where are you going?" I sprang back out of the seat I'd just taken.

"Supply closet down the hall. It has spare clothes."

Right. Shifter U had to keep extra pieces of unisex clothes in case of accidental shifting. Usually by the time they hit college age, most shifters had enough control not to shift by mistake, but there were some whose control wasn't as good. And sometimes, especially around the full moon or moments of high emotion—like during a fight—the change happened without warning.

"Maybe I better go with you." I hadn't forgotten about Mafia Hit Man and his buddy.

He narrowed his eyes at me. "I'm not helpless."

Waving my hands in surrender, I sank into the chair. After he'd left, I took a moment to check out his office. Again, he surprised me. I'd expected the space to be neat and organized. For someone who followed such a stringent schedule, his office was pretty chaotic. Books were piled on every flat surface, with files and notebooks shoved here and there at random. A plant of some kind, one with trailing vines, sat in the corner, half its leaves dead or dying. There wasn't anything personal, though. No framed pictures, no knickknacks.

Even the screen saver on his computer was generic. No personality anywhere to be found.

I couldn't handle the poor dying plant. I popped back out of the chair and reached for the planter. The soil in the pot was as dry as the Wyoming plains in August. I didn't see any water in the office. I'd have to get some before I left campus. I started picking dead leaves off the vines. "You need to take better care of this," I said when I heard the door open behind me.

"I'd appreciate it if you didn't touch my stuff." Though his tone was calm, the mix of scents emanating from him indicated a combination of emotions that were anything but calm. Irritation was there, along with a dash of suspicion. But nearly overwhelming his odor completely was the musky smell of lust. It washed over me, and my hands trembled on one of the crispy leaves.

I shrugged, then tossed the dead leaves into a wastebasket by the desk. "Don't blame me when your plant dies," I said, trying to sound as unaffected as he did. He was better at it.

He dropped the stack of cotton onto the chair I'd deserted.

I don't know what got into me—maybe it was the cool way he watched me despite the strong emotions I could smell—but I decided to enact a little revenge. Facing away from him, I pulled the sweater off and took my time folding it, as though the fate of the world rested on the perfect alignment of seams. It might have been my imagination, and admittedly I had an active one, but I was sure I felt the laser-like heat of his stare on my ass. I twisted to place the sweater on his desk, making sure the move accentuated the muscles of my abs and back.

He grunted. It took everything in me to not check out his expression.

I grabbed the sweatpants from the top of the pile and made a show of bending over to step into first one leg, then the other. I might not have been porno material, but I had a decent ass. And I was working with an appreciative audience. Heat and musk blew through the room.

"You're playing a dangerous game, pup."

My stomach lurched in one of those giddy, almost-but-not-quite uncomfortable sensations. Anyone else who called me pup would have felt my fangs. I don't deal well with condescension. But from him… my insides squirmed.

I bit my lip but quit playing. I hitched the pants up over my hips and then tugged the T-shirt on without fanfare. The tension in the room lessened a couple of notches. I dropped into the guest chair again. With a barely audible sigh, William took his own seat behind his desk.

"So, you going to tell me what today was all about? Why a couple of creeps are tracking you all over town?"

It was as if the last couple of minutes hadn't happened. He'd managed to tamp down every bit of heat and intensity. He sat calmly behind his desk, his face a mask of control, and not even his scent belied his emotions. How in the hell did he do that? Maybe there was an annex class or something I could take? It would be a useful skill to have. I didn't like being on the other end of it, though.

William clasped his hands together on the cluttered desktop. "I appreciate the efforts you took, but you need to stay out of it. I can handle it from here."

I leaned back and crossed my arms over my chest. "Really?"

"It'll be safer for everyone—you especially—if they don't connect you to me."

This time the condescending words, far from making my insides squirm, pissed me off. "You know, I'm not a kid. I can take care of myself. Hell, today I kept you safe."

"I don't question your abilities. These are not people you want to mess around with."

I narrowed my eyes at him. "And if they show up at Buddy's again?"

He pressed his lips into a thin line before answering. "It is unlikely that they'll make another appearance. I intend to take care of this before they have a chance to make a nuisance of themselves."

"Nuisance? These guys aren't trying to sell magazine subscriptions door-to-door. I'm pretty sure they have something more violent in mind."

"I'll take care of it." He sat at his desk, implacable. "Now, you'd better go. I have work to do." He straightened a stack of papers in front of him.

Stupid, stubborn man. I stood. "This isn't over."

"It is for you."

I grinned at him. "Yeah, good luck with that. I don't take orders too well." With that oddly satisfying statement, I strolled out of his stuffy, impersonal office.

Chapter Three

"IT'S been five days." I glared at Ford, who was inventorying the café's supply of flavored syrups like nothing was wrong. Didn't he understand what was at stake here?

"Uh-huh." He made a note on the clipboard in front of him. "Are you going to help with this? Month-end isn't the best time for you to mentally check out."

I was leaning against the counter, staring morosely into the empty dining area. Granted, it was midnight, so the room should have been empty. Ford and I were there to do the month-end inventory and food cost reports.

Ford looked up from his counts and glared at me. Oh yeah. I should have been counting too. But how was I supposed to concentrate on tallying coffee stirrers when William had been a complete no-show for the last five days? He hadn't set foot in the café since the day those weird city slickers showed up. Five whole days. Was he pissed? Did he leave town? Was he dead? I didn't know because he wasn't here when he was supposed to be.

"What if he's dead?"

"He isn't dead." Ford rolled his eyes.

"He might be. You don't know. Those creeps with the stupid bolo ties might have found him, killed him, and buried his lifeless body in a shallow grave."

"Don't be melodramatic. He's not dead. He's probably just busy."

"But it's been five days. He's never been gone this long."

Ford tucked back a glossy black strand of hair. "Maybe your superstalking got on his nerves and he decided it was time to avoid you."

"Jerk." I hitched myself up to sit on the counter. Then I bit my lip. "You don't really think he's avoiding me, do you?"

"Damn it, Donnie. If you're not going to help, at least let me work in peace. I don't want to be here until dawn. I have to open in the morning too. I don't have time for this."

Ford was right. But he didn't have to be so crabby about it. I was just… itchy. Kind of like how I'd felt before my first shift. My body was preparing for *something*. For a change. For action. Problem was, I didn't know what it was preparing for. I'd give almost anything for it to be hormones. Sex was easy. And after my adventures the other day, sexual frustration was a real concern. But this… this was something else.

Restlessness.

"Shit," I muttered, jumping off the counter. "You're right. I'm not going to be good for anything tonight. Tell you what. You finish inventory tonight, and I'll open for you in the morning. That way you can get a little extra sleep. I can't seem to settle."

Ford set the clipboard down, concern flashing across his face. "Dude, you okay?"

I shrugged, trying to shake the invisible weight from my shoulders. "I'm fine. I need to run or something." Track down that stubborn, sexy excuse for a mountain of a man and knock some sense into him. Or at least make sure he was alive. Whichever.

"Do yourself a favor and don't go looking for William. Let it—him—go."

Damn. It was like Ford could read my mind.

"Sure thing," I said absently, planning my attack.

THE last time I wandered campus in the middle of the night, I was nineteen, drunk, and trying to figure out how I was going to get Brandon Carter naked. Tonight I was twenty-two, stone sober, and trying to figure out the best way to track a surly college professor. Oh, and I was in my coyote form, carrying a grocery bag with shorts, a T-shirt, and flip-flops in my teeth. If I found William, I didn't want to deal with the distraction of being naked.

This wasn't the smartest idea I'd ever had. I was going to try to sniff out a shifter, one of the hundreds who regularly roamed this campus. Even if by some miracle I was able to pick up William's unique scent, it could lead me in circles around the social sciences building as easily as it could lead me to his home. For all I knew, he lived twenty miles away and commuted to the school every day.

Leaves rustled nearby and I crouched, senses straining. Giggling erupted from a bush, and I spied a

couple of coeds stumbling their way back to the dorms. I
didn't need my shifter-enhanced nose to pick up the aroma
of alcohol wafting from them.

I darted past, keeping to the shadows. It would
be hard to keep a low profile with a couple of girls
shrieking about a wild animal carrying a grocery sack
on campus.

When I reached Harmon Hall—the building where
William's office was located—I cast about, trying to
pick up his scent. Unfortunately he spent a lot of time
going in and out of this building, so finding his scent
wasn't the problem. Not tracking the scent in circles
was much more problematic. Damn, the guy must have
walked everywhere. One tantalizing scent trail led to
the commons building. Another led to the athletics
building. The one place that sagebrush-and-herb smell
didn't lead to was a parking lot. Which was a relief. It
meant he really did walk everywhere. If he'd driven,
I'd never be able to trail him past the parking lot.

Finally, after what felt like hours, I found a line of
eau de William that was stronger than the rest, heading
west and away from Harmon Hall, past the commons
building toward downtown. At first I was afraid this was
only the path he took to Buddy's—back when he still
came to Buddy's, the jerk—but it branched off a couple
of blocks from the café. I slunk past the stone entrance
of a subdivision and found myself facing a brick town
house with a long expanse of lawn behind it.

Hm. I didn't figure William for the town house
type. I guess I thought he was more rustic than that. Log
cabin, maybe. Of course, that could be my lumberjack
fantasies coloring my imagination.

From the outside his house didn't have any more
personality than his office. It looked like every other

house in the subdivision. The same redbrick façade. The same perfectly manicured lawn. It was a far cry from the explosion of stuff that marked my parents' house. Even the apartment I shared with Ford was less generic.

Headlights flashed at the end of the street, so I ducked behind an evergreen bush in front of William's neighbor's house. The vehicle moved slowly, stopping in front of each of the identical mailboxes. Two men were silhouetted by the dashboard lights, and I saw their shadowy forms lean forward at each house, as though they were looking for something. Or someone.

Somehow I didn't think they were pizza delivery people.

A dog barked down the street, and the car drove out of the subdivision at a more normal speed.

I was getting paranoid. Probably a couple of guys visiting an old friend. At three in the morning. Right.

I looked at what I assumed was William's house. It didn't appear as though anyone was awake inside. Of course, it *was* three in the morning. Normal people, even gorgeous manly men, were probably asleep. I dashed from shadow to shadow until I stood in front of his property.

I was debating whether to shift, ring the doorbell, and demand answers from William—I still hadn't confirmed whether he was actually alive yet—when I heard footsteps echoing lightly down the street. Two men. Both in all black. Nope, nothing suspicious about that at all.

The breeze shifted, and the distinctive smell of urban decay and violence assaulted my sensitive nose.

I growled low in my throat.

I hunkered down behind the evergreen bush in front of William's house—the twin to the one I'd hidden behind in his neighbor's yard—to watch the men. One crept up the two steps to William's porch, and the other faced the street. The first guy, Mafia Hit Man based on the nasty odor, pulled something the size of a checkbook from his back pocket and selected a skinny metal tool. He knelt in front of the door. Seriously? He was picking the lock?

I had to do something. I couldn't sit back and watch a couple of big-city creeps break into William's house and murder him while he slept. Assuming he was still alive, which, since these guys were still trying to get to him, seemed likely. Mafia Hit Man shifted, and moonlight glinted off something in his belt. Crap on a cracker, Mafia dude had a gun. I was a forty-five-pound coyote. I didn't stand much of a chance against that.

The doorknob turned under Mafia Hit Man's hand. The time for dithering was up. I burst from my hiding spot, growling and snarling. Mafia Hit Man stumbled back, crashing into Balding Blond Guy and knocking him to the ground. Score!

Mafia Hit Man steadied, reaching for his gun. I charged forward and latched on to his arm, sinking my sharp teeth through his long-sleeved black shirt and into flesh.

Something primal surged through me at the taste of his blood on my tongue. Sure, I'd killed a rabbit or pheasant or two while running around as a coyote, but this was different, stronger. Satisfying. I was protecting my mate from those who would do him harm. It was all very… *alpha*. How cool was that?

Holy shit. Did I just think *mate*?

My jaw loosened in surprise, and when the dude tried to pull away, I focused back on the situation at hand. I growled and bit down harder.

I'd lost track of Balding Blond Guy while I tore into Mafia Hit Man. Big mistake. Pain roared through me even as I heard the muffled pop of a gun. Balding Blond Guy had struggled to his feet and managed to pull his own gun free.

Fuck, that hurt.

The bullet scored across my shoulder, sending waves of fire along my side and down my foreleg. I yelped, releasing my jaws' hold on Mafia Hit Man.

Balding Blond Guy leveled his gun for another shot. I was screwed. There was no way I could get away in time. Nowhere I could go.

A porch light a couple of houses down flared to life, and someone shouted, "Hey, what's going on over there?"

Balding Blond Guy shoved his gun into his belt, reached down to haul Mafia Hit Man to his feet, and dragged him away. They stumbled down the street in the opposite direction from the nosy neighbor.

I hunched back, preparing to lunge after them, burning gunshot wound be damned, but a large hand clamped on the ruff of my neck and hauled me bodily into the warm, sagebrush-scented town house of a very angry shifter.

Chapter Four

I YIPPED in protest. Damn it, that hurt. Didn't the stupid man realize I'd been shot? Shot protecting his sorry ass, no less. I sat back on my haunches and glared up at a very large, glowering William. Those long, muscular arms were crossed over a very wide, very naked chest. Man, he was yummy.

"What the hell are you playing at?"

I didn't have to take that kind of attitude. I narrowed my eyes at him and prepared to leave. My shoulder, unfortunately, chose that moment to tell me just how hurt it really was. The adrenaline had worn off, leaving behind a flaming ball of agony. I couldn't suppress the pained whine that escaped.

William dropped his arms and bent toward me. Instinct had me scooting away from him. I didn't really think he'd hurt me, but I was injured, and that was enough for my coyote to use caution.

"You're hurt." William didn't move any closer. He probably recognized my withdrawal for what it was.

Duh. I'd have given anything to say it out loud. Did he think the blood soaking my coat was a fashion accessory? Unfortunately my canine anatomy wasn't conducive to human speech. I rolled my eyes instead. We'd struggled with the nonverbal communication before, but maybe William would get it this time.

He straightened and propped his hands on his hips. "Can you shift?"

Another myth about shapeshifters was that we could magically heal from an injury by shifting into our other form. Sadly it wasn't the cure-all fiction would have us believe. All shifting would do was allow someone to treat human-me instead of coyote-me.

I closed my eyes, trying to focus past the pain and the knowledge of just how much this was going to suck. I counted backward from five in a useless bid to prepare myself. Changing doesn't hurt, but changing with a bullet wound would put unnatural pressure on the area. In other words, ouch.

I sucked in a breath, then *shifted.*

It took a little longer than normal. Not quite instantaneous. And the effort left me sweating and gasping. Stupid men with their stupid bullets.

William crouched next to me. He brushed my bangs out of my eyes, and that simple caress made my insides go wonky. It was so gentle, his fingers so warm. I blinked up at him, and all the things I wanted to say to him about stubborn men and rough handling got caught in my throat at the concern on his face. Instead I blurted out, "You're not dead."

He rocked back on his heels. "No, I'm not."

"Where have you been?"

"Around." He stood. "I'll get a towel. You're bleeding all over my floor."

I watched him leave the living room, muttering under my breath, "Yeah, let's worry about the generic wood laminate rather than the *bullet wound* in my back." I sat up, wincing as the burning sensation increased. I peeked over my shoulder. Blood smeared along my side. The metallic scent of it made my stomach roil. The blood of my prey—appetizing. My own blood—nauseating. It was true what they said. You did learn something new every day.

I twisted my shoulder, trying to get a closer look at the wound. The bullet had left a shallow furrow about six inches long. I pressed along the edges, hissing at the pain but relieved that the bleeding seemed to have slowed. It didn't look like it would need stitches, thankfully. Stitches would mean I couldn't shift again until they were removed, at least not without them being ripped from my skin in the process.

"Don't play with it," William commanded, striding back into the room, a towel in one hand and a first aid kit in the other. Sadly he'd pulled on a worn flannel shirt along the way.

"It's fine," I said. It occurred to me, once again, I was stark naked in front of William. It wasn't that I objected to naked, but I generally preferred it if the nudity came with some sexy times. "Any chance you can grab my clothes? I've got a bag tucked away under your neighbor's bushes."

He raised an eyebrow at that, but he settled to the floor next to me instead of heading out for my clothes.

"Sit on this towel. I'll clean out the wound. We'll find out if you need to visit the ER or not."

"Or not," I said. "Throw a bandage on it. I'll be fine."

"I'll be the judge of that."

Sometimes I really liked his commanding tone. Sometimes it made me want to throttle him. Two guesses as to how I felt this time. I wanted to tell him *You're not the boss of me*, but that would make me sound about eleven, and I really, really didn't want him to see me as a kid.

His movements were efficient, though surprisingly gentle, as he cleaned the blood from my back and probed the wound. "This is going to burn," he warned, only seconds before he poured acid down my shoulder. Okay, it was really some kind of noxious antiseptic, but from the way it burned, I'd have sworn it contained some caustic chemical. I hissed and jerked away, but William's big hand held me in place while the evil solution did its job. I focused on the heat of his palm, the strength of his fingers rather than the bubbling, stinging disinfectant.

"Why were you out there tonight?" He dabbed at the wound with a square of gauze. His other hand still rested on my shoulder, and his thumb began to trace the edge of my shoulder blade. The touch warmed me, and I wanted to settle into it, extend the contact. Then his question registered.

"I came to find out if you were okay."

"Of course I'm okay."

"You haven't been to Buddy's in five days. You never go that long between visits."

"I thought it better to lie low for a while. I didn't want you caught up in my problems again."

I snorted. "Yeah, that didn't happen."

"Clearly." His tone was dry, but I thought I detected a bit of humor in it. Humor was good, right?

"So, you going to tell me who they are now? And why these guys have such a hard-on for you?"

"I thought we agreed you were going to stay out of it." William spread some kind of ointment on the injury.

"No, you agreed. Besides, in case you didn't figure it out, I saved your ass again. Who knows what those guys would have done if they'd gotten in."

"I was prepared." William pressed a clean pad of gauze over my wound before taping the edges.

I snorted. Again. It was either that or burst out with "ha!" and that seemed a little melodramatic.

He released my shoulder and used his hand to tilt my head toward the door. My jaw dropped. A bank vault was less secure. There were laser sensors, some kind of computerized locking mechanism, four monitors displaying the yard, driveway, and porch, and no fewer than *three* deadbolts. Of course, after the fancy locking mechanisms, the deadbolts were probably overkill.

"Who are you?" He was like James Bond or that guy from *Mission: Impossible.* "Normal people don't booby-trap their doors."

"You know who I am. I'm a professor at Cody College."

"Yeah, and I'm Wile E. Coyote." I scooted to the monitors and took in the different views. "So you knew they were there the whole time?"

"Yes."

"Why didn't you call the cops?"

"The cops around here aren't prepared for men like that."

Every word he spoke added to my confusion and my desperate need to *know*. "What the hell are you involved in?"

"None of your business."

The burning wound in my shoulder said otherwise. "Fuck that. I got shot trying to save your ass. I think that earns me some kind of explanation."

"You wouldn't have gotten shot at if you'd minded your own business."

"If you hadn't been avoiding me, I wouldn't have had to track you down in the first place."

"That's a circular argument," he said, crossing his arms over his chest. Even sitting on the floor, he managed to intimidate.

"Yeah, well, it's all I got." I turned away from the monitors and realized—again—that I was naked. "Really, William, could you bring my clothes in? I'm sure my arguments will be much more valid if my junk isn't hanging out."

His eyes glinted and his lips twitched, an aborted smile, probably. "I'm kind of enjoying the view."

I straightened to my full five feet ten inches—or, well, as much as I could while sitting down—and propped my fists at my hips. "Not fair. You're trying to distract me, and it isn't going to work. I want answers, and I want them now. This... is...." My voice trailed off because William leaned forward, pressing close until there was barely an inch between us. My breath caught and my bones melted. They simply dissolved right then and there. My senses were full of William, in the heat emanating from his body, in the scent drifting off him. He traced his thumb from my chin, down past my Adam's apple, until it pressed lightly in the hollow at the base of my throat. "So not fair," I whispered.

"What's not fair?" His deep voice rumbled in my chest. He bent his head, and his beard tickled my skin as he nuzzled my neck.

I licked suddenly dry lips and focused on breathing. "This. That." I lassoed my runaway thoughts. What was I saying? Oh, yeah. "You can't use sex to distract me." I totally deserved some credit for getting the words out. I was pretty sure they were in English, but I wouldn't have staked my life on it or anything.

I tilted my head back to give him more room to explore. He took me up on it immediately, nibbling up the tendon in my neck to the sensitive skin behind my ear. I closed my eyes and sighed.

Sleeping with him wouldn't make me a slut, right? And if it did, did I care? As his hands snaked up my flanks, I thought *Maybe not.*

Damn, this attraction I had to him was out of control. "You're not just doing this to distract me, right?"

"Maybe." I swore I felt him smile against my ear. "Is it working?"

Before I could formulate an answer, he bit my earlobe, just hard enough to send lightning to my groin. I had a point to make, I was sure of it. But this… this completely blanked my mind of anything but the feel, the smell of him.

I wrapped my arms around his neck, pressing hard against him. I hitched a leg around his hips and pulled up far enough to align our groins. "Fine. Go ahead and distract me."

I knew distraction really was his goal. I even knew I should be a little offended that he thought it would be that easy. But, man, after months of wishing, of wanting, I was absolutely going to let myself be distracted. "Promise you'll respect me in the morning?" I teased.

"Maybe." He nipped and nibbled his way from ear to neck to shoulder. Goose bumps followed in the wake of his teeth.

"Stop." I wriggled away from him. Not far—not after finally getting something I'd dreamed of for months—but I needed a couple of inches.

He cocked his head, and a flash of uncertainty crossed his face.

"Don't worry, handsome." I smoothed my fingers along his jaw. "This is like my birthday and Christmas combined. I finally get to unwrap my manly man." His lips twitched under my fingers, the start of a smile he hid by leaning forward and pressing his mouth to mine.

Damn, the man could kiss. Strong lips, silky beard. Possessive. Claiming. I forgot my desire to undress him and instead focused on the merging of our mouths. The slick glide of his tongue against mine, the way he sucked my bottom lip between his teeth. A couple of minutes later, I had to pull back because I needed more oxygen than the few gasping breaths I'd managed.

I gripped the flaps of his tan-and-light-blue flannel shirt, the ones that framed his truly amazing chest. "Just lie back and, I don't know, think of England. I've got some exploring to do."

He snorted out a laugh but did as I asked. Well, he lay back. I hoped he wasn't thinking of England, not while I straddled his waist, naked and so turned on I could barely think. The rough/soft texture of his jeans stroked my thighs, and I rocked a little, thrilling at the pressure against my seriously straining dick. No, I couldn't go there yet. Even without trying, he distracted me.

I spread the fabric of his shirt to the sides, the better to examine every inch of him. How in the hell did a college professor get so built? I doubted lifting textbooks was responsible for the bulk of his pecs. Or shoulders. Or, hell, all of him. I didn't think I was shallow, but his was a form I could ogle dreamily for hours. Days, even.

His abs flexed, and my fingers itched to touch each and every defined slab of muscle. I wanted to comb through the thick pelt of chest hair and the arrowing trail that pointed south.

"Are you only going to look?"

William's rumbling voice broke through my mesmerization. Oh, right. I could touch him now.

I started with light touches, letting the sensitive pads of my fingers barely graze his hot flesh. He squirmed a little, both trying to escape and push into the caress at the same time. William was ticklish. Who'd have thought? When I scraped one of his nipples with the edge of my thumb, he gasped, the dusky peak tightening into a sharp point.

I leaned forward, tongue darting out to tease the bud. A lick, a flick; I was careful to keep the touch light.

William grabbed one of my hands, pushing it solidly into his chest, and arched underneath me, pressing his cock against my ass. "Don't tease," he growled.

How did I tell him it wasn't a matter of teasing, that it was really a matter of being sidetracked by the glory of him below me and the niggling fear that this was some kind of dream I'd wake up from if I made an incautious move? Nope, I couldn't tell him that. So, instead, I decided to focus. And maybe tease a little.

"Fine." I bounced a bit, making him grunt. "I suppose I could stop altogether."

"Don't you dare. I've waited too long for this." He sat up using only the muscles of his abs—a feat I heartily approved of—and I had to adjust my seat to keep from falling back.

He tossed aside his shirt, then wrapped his beefy arms around me, dragging me closer. The new position— and, well, gravity—had our lower bodies grinding against each other. My hands gripped convulsively at his shoulders and my hips thrust, increasing the pressure and the pleasure.

"Pants," I gasped, undulating in his lap. I reached between us and undid the button; then I tugged the tab of the zipper down. Almost immediately, William's cock fell hard and heavy into my hand. I wrapped my fingers around it, squeezing gently. William grunted, surging in my grip. I stroked his length, base to tip. Each time my fingers brushed against the underside of the head, William cursed and rocked into my hold. It was the sexiest fucking thing I'd ever seen, and I could have kept going for hours.

William had other ideas. He reached his hand down and gripped my dick. He mirrored my motions, and soon we were a pumping, humping tangle of fingers and cocks. I don't know when it happened, but soon William laced my fingers with his, and our joined hands were wrapped around both our erections, stroking fast and hard. The combination of his fingers, the dick-on-dick friction, and the pure eroticism of the moment all culminated in an epic orgasm. My balls drew tight, and electricity zinged through my body. I fell forward and bit William's shoulder as I erupted. Time was a vague, hazy concept, but I don't think more than a couple of seconds passed before William came, spilling over our cocks and fingers.

I LAY sprawled across him, chin resting on my hands, which were in turn resting on his furry chest. I was completely sated but not sleepy. Like my muscles were made of chicken noodle soup, but my brain was wired on Red Bull. To his credit, William hadn't fallen into unconsciousness the minute we were done either. Part of my overactive brain wondered if that was because it hadn't been nearly as earth-shattering for him as it was for me. The rest of my brain—and every inch of my extremely satisfied body—knew better.

I wasn't sure he was aware of it, but his hand kept running up and down my spine, as though he were petting me. He paused, tracing the edge of the gauze he'd applied. "You sore?"

"Nah. Endorphins. I'm not feeling any pain right now." I winked up at him.

His expression was serious, almost tender. "I don't like seeing you hurt."

I shrugged, ignoring the twinge it caused. "It's a scrape."

"It's more than a scrape," he insisted.

"Not by much."

He was silent for a minute. Then he said, "When I saw you on the monitors, fighting those guys, I didn't think I'd be able to get to you in time." He growled low in his throat. "Don't do that again. I don't think I can handle it."

I held my breath. He was serious. And he'd said something earlier about waiting for this. "Does that mean you actually like me?" I tried to keep my voice teasing, but I'd bet good money he saw through my attempt.

I could see the struggle in his face, the closed eyes and the pursed lips, but to my relief, he answered. "I've been watching you for months. Of course I like you. Everybody likes you."

I pressed my head to my arms so he wouldn't see my expression. I'd wished, though I feared it was closer to wishful thinking, that William might eventually come to care about me. Saying he liked me was a far cry from undying love and devotion, but it was more than I'd expected at this point. And he'd been watching me? I bit my forearm to keep from shouting in happiness.

"You have no idea. Seeing you every day, watching and listening to the way you interact with people. You've got a good heart."

Hope spread through me, a dangerous thing. It was time for me to change the subject before I made a complete idiot of myself.

"William?" I asked, curling my fingers into the hair on his chest. I'm pretty sure that was the only bit of muscle control I had left at that point.

"Hm?" His hand slowed its caress of my back, but only for a moment.

"What's your shift?"

He combed his fingers through my hair, pushing back the strands that hung in front of my eyes. "American bison."

I shoved myself up, doing a makeshift push-up on his broad chest. "What? You're a buffalo?"

"American bison," he corrected, pressing his lips into a disapproving line.

"Same thing." Then it hit me. I drew my knees up until I straddled his waist. "Oh my God. William. Bill. You're Buffalo Bill!"

Now he scowled, an act that should have looked intimidating but, given our current situation, just made him look adorable. "Don't call me Bill."

I tried. Really I did. But I couldn't control the laughter the rolled out of me. "Oh my God, what were your parents thinking?"

"It's a family name." He sat up, and I adjusted to keep from falling. I liked the way we felt, naked skin to naked skin. I wasn't losing this seat for anything.

"Are you related to him?"

Now he just looked offended. "Hardly. He was a bison hunter. Bison shifters do not hunt bison."

I wrapped my arms around his neck and leaned in to nibble at his frowning lips. "Did you play football? Maybe somewhere in New York?"

He rubbed his silky beard against my smooth cheek. "I'm going to regret telling you that, aren't I?"

"Oh, were you named after the guy in *The Silence of the Lambs*?"

He huffed. "If you're not going to let it go, then I guess I need to distract you." He rolled, pressing me back against the wood flooring.

I grinned. "Have I mentioned I really, really like the way you distract me?"

He scooted down my body, trailing his mouth down my throat and to my chest. "Yeah?"

"Yeah." I groaned as his lips and tongue started doing erotic things to my body that emptied my brain of any coherent thought. "Absolutely. But maybe we can move this to the bedroom? Maybe somewhere softer than the floor?"

Chapter Five

WILLIAM didn't exactly push me out the door the next morning. He didn't have to. My cell phone pinged at me a couple of hours after we'd moved to his bed, exhausted from round three. My body ached in the best way possible—maybe we'd have to reconsider the whole sex-on-the-floor thing—and it took me longer than it should have to stumble out of bed and into the living room to find my grocery bag of clothes, which also held my cell phone. I'd finally convinced William to grab my stuff in the break between rounds two and three.

Only my promise to Ford to cover the café's opening kept me from crawling back onto William's soft king-size mattress and snuggling into his brawny arms. Buffalo shifter was my new favorite pillow.

I dug out my phone and turned off the alarm. It wasn't worth getting dressed, since I'd only have to change back to coyote to run home and dress for work. The shift would pull painfully on my injured shoulder, but it wouldn't be unbearable. Besides, it would take too long to walk on two feet, and no way was I calling Ford. I debated waking William up before I left. On the one hand, he probably needed sleep. He hadn't even twitched when my alarm went off. On the other hand, though, it was rude to dash out without a word the morning after a night of amazing sex. Unless it was a one-off or a booty call. I bit my lip. What if William thought it was a one-off?

A glance at the door told me that, regardless of the status of our undefined relationship—how should a guy refer to a series of random interactions with the man of his dreams?—I'd have to wake him up. No way in hell was I going to attempt to get past the *Mission: Impossible* hardware on the door. They probably had some kind of self-destruct mechanism.

I stood in the doorway to William's bedroom and stared at his sleeping form. His dark, curly hair stuck out in the craziest mop of bedhead I'd ever seen. Which was an odd contrast to the serious expression his face held, even in sleep.

"I can feel your stare." He hadn't twitched or altered his breathing in any way. Nothing to indicate he was awake. "Sneaking away?" His eyes popped open, and he pushed himself into a sitting position. The white sheet pooled at his waist, and it was all I could do to stop from crawling back into bed with him.

I adjusted the shopping bag of clothes to cover my groin. "Uh, no. I mean, yeah, sort of." I cleared my throat and tried again. "I have to get to work, and I didn't want to wake you up. You were sleeping, or so I thought. But then I saw the door and realized I had no idea how any of your locks and gadgets work." Why were mornings after so damn awkward?

"Of course." He scratched his beard, yawning. He motioned to the grocery sack. "Were you going to get dressed first?"

"Actually, no." I rocked from foot to foot. "It'll be faster if I run in my shifted form, and I don't have much time."

He looked over at his alarm clock. "It's only four-thirty."

"I promised Ford—you remember him from Buddy's, right?—to open this morning since I made him do the overnight inventory. And we open at five. Which means I've got to haul ass if I want to make it on time."

"I'll take you." He flipped the sheet back, revealing the rest of his muscled body.

I tried, really I did, to keep my eyes above his neck. Not that I hadn't examined every inch of him the night before, but it seemed rude to ogle a man first thing in the morning. Even if the guy sported a morning erection. Maybe especially if the guy sported a morning erection.

"Donnie?"

I shook my head, only then realizing William had been saying something to me while I fixated on his naked body. "No. Ah, I mean, I need to run. Clear my head."

He rose and walked to the dresser. I just stood there, incapable of making a move or a sound. Jesus. Normally I couldn't shut my brain off, but sometimes around him, I just blanked out. Such a dangerous habit. He pulled on a pair of boxers and turned toward me. His lips twitched into an almost smile. My dopey expression probably amused him.

I closed my eyes, then took a deep breath to clear my head. "Um, yeah. Can you open the door for me?"

I couldn't figure out what he was thinking as he led the way to the living room. I wasn't sure what *I* was thinking, come to that. Last night had been pretty spectacular—mind-blowing, even—but it left me in an emotional limbo. Stupid questions like *When will I see him again?* or *Will I see him again?* and *Does he even want to see me again?* cycled through my brain. I didn't ask any of them. Sometimes my brain-mouth filter was absent, but no way was I putting those thoughts into the atmosphere.

He picked up on them anyway. "We can't do this again."

I froze, only a little surprised at the stabbing pain his words created. I should have expected it. I also should have let it go, but I'd never been too dedicated to *should*s. "Why not?"

"It's too dangerous."

"Dangerous," I said dully.

"You also need to stay out of my business."

Humiliation and hurt swamped me. Hurt that he could so easily push me away after what happened last night. Humiliation that last night really had been about distracting me from whatever he was involved in.

I couldn't form the words I wanted to say, words that would let him know just how much of a bastard I thought he was, so I went with silence.

He fiddled at the control panel. The door opened, and I let the shift take me. By the time I'd caught the handle of the plastic grocery sack between my teeth,

William had turned away. I watched his retreating form as the door closed between us.

Like so many times before, I'd let hope rather than reality color my emotions. Someday I'd learn the lesson. I whined deep in my throat and sped down the street, chasing the rising sun, trying to bury the trickles of shame winding through me.

I DIDN'T have a chance to shower if I wanted to make it to Buddy's on time, so I headed straight to the café. I shifted into my human form, raided Buddy's first aid kit to re-cover my shoulder wound, and pulled on the clothes from the night before. It was a good thing I could do the mundane opening tasks in my sleep, because my brain refused to focus. I was too caught up in the previous night. Not just the incredible sex but the whole thing. How could he show such tenderness and then dismiss me so easily the next morning? And to top it all off, I hadn't even gotten what I'd gone to his house to get.

Like the scene at the college, I got no answers.

And like the scene at the college, I was naked.

Maybe there was a correlation there? Next time I saw William, I was totally going to wear clothes.

And speaking of sex—since it so rarely left my brain when William was involved—what was last night? I mean, sure, I'd sort of resigned myself to it having been a onetime deal, but why? I'd done it because too much speculation and temptation had eroded my common sense. But why had William? Somehow I doubted his damn control had been worn away out of lust for me. And surely he'd never been tempted, especially by me, to ignore his common sense.

As humiliating as the realization was, I was convinced he really had been trying to distract me from my questions. Well, mission accomplished.

My bad mood lasted all morning. It was compounded by my throbbing shoulder, stupid mistakes, and pain-in-the-ass customers. Seriously, the customer may always be right, but they could also be asshats.

Ford came in about ten, just as I was apologizing to a snot-nosed college kid who was irritated that I'd forgotten the sprinkle of cinnamon on top of his extra-large triple soy latte with fat-free whip, two pumps of vanilla, and one of caramel—extra hot, of course. I wanted to point him to the local grocery store and its selection of instant flavored espresso drinks so he could be pretentious on his own time, but since I actually liked this job, I bit my tongue.

"You've got the counter," I snapped before Ford even had time to drop his backpack in the office. "I need to prep for lunch."

He raised an eyebrow but didn't say anything, and I stormed into the kitchen. Maybe a minute or two in the walk-in would cool my temper. The dented stainless-steel door opened with a protesting squeak that made my teeth ache. The stacks of cardboard- and plastic-covered pastries mocked me from their wire shelves. I'd been trying to convince Buddy for months that we needed to ditch the premade, microwave-ready pastries and sandwiches in favor of fresh-baked and made-from-scratch options. I knew for a fact my blueberry muffins were better than the frozen ones we popped in the oven each morning. And assembling a real sandwich wouldn't take any more time than one of those toaster-oven pseudo-paninis we offered. I was mortified every time a customer returned an Italian combo panini because it was still frozen on the inside. No pretending it was the real deal then.

Well, being manipulated so easily the night before by William was right up there on the humiliation scale. But that was as much my fault as William's. At least William hadn't pretended to be something he wasn't. All college professors secured their homes like Fort Knox, right?

I grabbed salad fixings from the walk-in cooler and dumped them on the prep table. The salads were fresh, at least, but not very creative. A handful of lettuce, a couple of tomato wedges, and a sprinkle of cheese was hardly a satisfying meal. I stacked the boring salads in their plastic containers and hauled them to the cooler display up front, where Ford was ringing in a sale. As soon as the customer left, Ford turned to me.

"What's eating you? You only bang shit around like that when you've had a run-in with your dad." He winged a dark eyebrow up in question.

"Not my dad." Squatting in front of the display, I arranged the plastic bowls and avoided making eye contact with Ford. The guy was too damn perceptive sometimes.

Through the glass backing of the case, I watched him cross his arms over his chest and close his eyes. "Damn it, Donnie. Tell me you didn't."

"Didn't what?" Pretending the exact placement of generic lettuce was of the utmost importance, I made sure each salad displayed the red skin of a tomato wedge.

"You slept with him."

My hands jerked, and three of the salads came crashing to the tiled floor in an explosion of iceberg lettuce. I glared at him, then at the floor. "Not cool, dude." I started scooping up lettuce and tomatoes.

"I can't believe you."

I ground my molars together and barely kept from growling. "Now's not a good time."

"What were you thinking?"

I flung a fistful of lettuce at him. "I said, not now." I surged to my feet and stalked to the back room so I could grab a broom.

When I returned to finish the cleanup, Ford was helping another customer. I'd dumped away the spoiled food when the café's doors opened and a familiar scent filled the room. I clenched my fist around the broom handle and squeezed my eyes shut. What was this? Pick on Donnie day?

James, my oldest brother, sauntered through the dining room with an arrogance that didn't match his dusty jeans and sweat-stained shirt. He, like my other two brothers and my father, always carried himself like he was the king of the world. I didn't get it. Not the why of it or the skill of it. Strangely, their personalities didn't quite match their swagger. They rarely acted like they were better than anyone else, and could always be counted on to give a hand. They were decent men.

But they were opinionated men, and their opinions about me and how I should live my life were the source of a bunch of conflict between us. Not the gay part. They didn't understand it, but they mostly ignored it, which was more than I could have said for some of my so-called friends in high school. Mostly I confused them. I wasn't satisfied to live the simple lives they lived. I didn't want the same things they wanted. And that confused the hell out of them.

Take James. He graduated high school, married a sweet coyote-shifter girl, got a job in the oil fields, and did his part to increase the coyote-shifter population. My second-oldest brother, Tim, did the same. My younger brother, Andy, the same. Then there was me. I graduated high school, enrolled in college, and got a job selling fancified—their word—coffee to coeds who didn't know any better. And, unless something completely cataclysmic happened, I was probably not going to usher in a new generation of coyote-shifter children.

Every couple of months, one of my brothers or my father would corner me to try to talk me into changing my citified—another of their words—ways. To be the coyote God and nature meant me to be.

"Baby bro!" James opened his arms wide for a hug that I stepped into. Hey, he might not understand me, but he was my brother, and we loved each other. And touch between shifter family members only reinforced those bonds.

"What brings you here?" I stepped back and shoved my hands into my pockets.

"I got some news and an opportunity for you." He glanced at one of the empty tables. "You got a minute?"

I bit my lip and thought about my options. This really wasn't a good time to have the same old conversation with James. But the way he said "news" made me think his news might be more than the typical bid to get me out into the oil fields. And, honestly, my brothers didn't make it past the city limits very often. I spent a lot of time with my nieces and nephews, but Dad, James, Tim, and Andy were usually working.

"I can't take a break," I said, finally deciding. "But you can come back to the kitchen with me while I finish lunch prep."

"Whatever works." He shrugged and followed me behind the counter. On the way I grabbed a cup and filled it with regular coffee with none of the "sissy" flavors my brother detested.

I handed the drink to him and led the way to the kitchen area. "What's up?"

He leaned against the stainless-steel counter, cradling the drink. "Janey is pregnant again."

I grinned and slapped his back. "Congrats. When's she due?" This would make baby number five for James and Janey. It'd been six years since their last, so I'd assumed they were done having kids.

"June. We're hoping for a girl. Janey says she's tired of dirt bikes and toy trucks."

I snorted. "I bet if you get a girl, she'll be just as into dirt bikes and toy trucks as the boys. You wouldn't know what to do with baby dolls and makeup. And when she starts dating? You'll scare away the boys with a shotgun."

James's face paled. "Oh shit."

"What?"

"Dating. I can't have a girl. I've been a boy. I know what goes through their minds. No way in hell can I let a daughter loose around teenage boys." He paused; then his face brightened. "Hey, maybe she'll be gay. Then I wouldn't have to worry about boys."

I choked. Never in a million years would I have predicted my brother would ever say such a thing. "There's a thought," I managed to croak through my spasming throat.

In an attempt to gain a little composure, I started re-creating the salads I'd dropped. This was not where I'd expected this conversation to go.

James shook his head like a big dog. "So, anyway, I was wondering if you could watch the kids on Friday night. I was thinking Janey and me could go out, have a little fun. We haven't had a date night in years, and with another baby coming, it might be a long time before we have another chance."

This was why I couldn't dislike my brother. He didn't understand me. He wanted to change me. But he was really a good guy at heart. He'd fallen for Janey when they were fourteen years old. Seriously, their names were James and Janey—clearly they were destined to be together. And despite coyotes' tendency to distractibility and short attention spans, his love for Janey and his family defied his instinct. All of my brothers, in fact, seemed to be as dedicated to their wives. It wasn't always the case. Most of my cousins were the definition of *love 'em and leave 'em*.

Part of me had been looking for something like what my brothers had with their wives. Maybe that was why, when I felt that connection to William, I pushed so hard.

"Of course," I said, mentally rearranging my weekend plans, which wasn't hard. It was Ford's turn to close on Friday, and all I'd intended to do was go back and forth between doing laundry at the laundromat and hassling Ford at the café. Anything was better than the laundromat, even four kids under the age of ten. "What time do you need me there?"

"Six?" James lifted a packet of raspberry vinaigrette salad dressing and sneered at it. If he was ever forced to eat a salad—God forbid!—he ate it with ranch or blue cheese. He definitely wouldn't be caught with *pink* dressing.

"Cool. I'll be there. Tell Janey not to feed them. I'll bring ingredients for homemade pizza. They should have fun with that." Yes, homemade pizza with four little kids was definitely better than laundry. And maybe I'd also be able to get my mind off the burly, manly man I'd been obsessing about for months. Maybe. Hopefully.

"That's great, man." James dropped the offending packet of dressing and propped his hands on his hips.

"Look, there was something else I wanted to run past you." His voice lost the grateful brother tone, smoothly transitioning into serious brother mode.

I popped the clear plastic top onto the salad bowl and took a quick, fortifying breath. I so knew where this was going.

"Lloyd Harrison—you remember him, right?— retired. Dad's going to be promoted to operations chief, and I'm moving up to crew chief in the oil fields."

"Great!" I interjected, hoping to distract him from his next sentence. "Congratulations."

Sadly, he wasn't deterred. "Yeah, thanks. It creates a hole, though, in the western field. We could really use you. Pay's decent, hours are steady. You'd be a shoo-in, what with the family history and all."

"I don't think—"

"Aren't you tired of this yet? Serving fancy coffee to college kids? Making minimum wage?"

"James." I sighed and tried to figure out, for the thousandth time, how to explain it to him. "I like my job. I'm good at it."

"Of course you are. Any fifteen-year-old could do it. But it's time you grew up. You can't do this forever."

I dragged my hand through my hair. "I don't intend to do it forever. But until I find something better—better for me," I stressed before he could bring up the oil field job again, "I'll stick with what I enjoy."

He shook his shaggy head. "I don't get it. You've always thought you were too good for real, honest work. Always looking for bigger and better things. Wasted your time and a crapload of money at college. There's nothing wrong with working with your hands, putting in an honest day's work. What are you waiting for? A bus ticket to New York City? You think you'd be happy in some city, surrounded by all those people?"

Frustration bubbled up inside me. "I have never thought I was better than you or anybody else. Just because I want something different than sweating away my days on an oil rig doesn't mean I'm ready to hightail it off to New York."

"Come on, you with your fancy cakes and organic salads."

So, apparently liking a little diversity in my diet meant I was jonesing for the big city. James was never going to get it. I bit my tongue before I could say something I'd regret. I had to remind myself I did, indeed, love my brother, and this particular argument wasn't going to be resolved today. "Look, James, I need to get back to work. I know you don't understand my job, but it is my job. I'll see you on Friday."

He grabbed his cup of coffee, took a swig, then set it down. "One of these days, Donnie, you'll have to get your act together. I just hope for your sake it's not too late." He strode out of the cramped kitchen space.

I counted to ten. Then I counted to ten again. It didn't help. "*Argh!*" I swept my arm out and knocked the newly prepared, still-boring salads to the ground. Staring at the bits of green and red produce scattered across the beige-tiled floor, I started laughing. No, it wasn't funny, but if I didn't laugh, I'd probably scream. Again.

Chapter Six

URBAN decay and gunpowder hit me bare seconds before the cold voice did. "You lied to us, Mr. Granger."

My hand clenched around the banana pepper I'd been examining. Friday night in the produce department at the local grocery store was the last place I expected to run into Mafia Hit Man. I held my breath and turned to face him. He'd given up the hokey western apparel and looked much more at home in black slacks and a button-down black shirt. He still stood out like a cheerleader at a biker bar, but it was better than the starched jeans and bolo tie he'd worn the first time I'd seen him.

I took a deep breath to calm my frantically beating heart, and the scrape along my shoulder blade twinged. "Excuse me?" No one would have been more surprised than I was that my voice stayed steady. This close, Mafia Hit Man managed to loom over me, despite the fact that he was only a couple of inches taller than me. His stocky build and menacing glower made him seem bigger than he was.

"You told us you didn't know the man we were looking for."

"Right." I nodded and did my best to draw out the word so it sounded like I didn't know why he was bringing it up again. *Gotta keep it cool, Donnie.*

"We've talked to a lot of people who are sure they've seen him at Bucky's. And seen you drooling over him when he's there."

"Buddy's," I corrected. "And we get a lot of people in and out of the café every day. I can't be expected to remember each and every one of them."

Mafia Hit Man grabbed an ear of corn and examined it from silky top to stalky bottom. He pulled one strip of green husk down, revealing the yellow and white kernels. He glanced at me from under dark brows. "And do you flirt with all of your customers, so they don't stand out either?"

I shrugged. "What can I say? I like to flirt. And being friendly earns better tips."

He peeled back another portion of husk. He wiped away stray strands of silk, caressing the curved top of the ear in a way that was, frankly, disturbingly sexual. He stripped back the last of the husk. I couldn't tear my eyes away from the swipe of his thumb over the end, the glide of his hand down the length. My stomach lurched. Did he know he was jacking off an ear of corn? My lip curled involuntarily, so I bit down on it to try to hide my reaction.

"Well, I've got a tip for you. You should think *long* and *hard* about *coming* clean."

I knew they weren't deliberate, but his double entendres were really creeping me out. I watched his hands maneuver around the corn with the same horrified fascination people have at car accident scenes.

His hands dropped until he gripped the cob at roughly groin level. "Things will go better for you if you don't make us do things the hard way." His knuckles whitened as he strengthened his hold. "You won't like the hard way." With a sickening *snap*, he broke the ear of corn in half, letting the pieces fall to the ground. He brushed the lingering strands of silk off his fingers.

I couldn't help but hold my hands protectively in front of my crotch.

"I'll be in touch." He spun on one glossy loafered heel and strode out of the produce department.

I stared at the mangled corn on the floor.

A cart with a squeaky wheel rolled slowly by, pushed by an elderly woman with a plastic rain cap over her hair.

A stock boy unloaded boxes of bananas onto a display.

And I still stood there, God only knew how long, staring at the mangled corn on the floor, until my phone *bing*ed. I had fifteen minutes to get my groceries and head out of town to babysit my nephews. A glance at my empty shopping basket, which I'd dropped at some point in that freaky exchange with Mafia Hit Man, told me there wasn't going to be enough time for homemade pizza.

Oh, well. Frozen pizza had been good enough for us when I was a kid. Tombstone would be fine for my nephews.

Maybe not Tombstone. No need to tempt fate.
Fuck it. Fast-food chicken it was.

THE drive out of the Cody city limits was an exercise
in paranoia and general nausea. Every time a car got
closer than half a block away, I worried it was one of
the city thugs following me to my brother's house. It
didn't matter if it was a rusted-out pickup they probably
wouldn't be caught dead in or the old-school Cadillac
driven by some blue-haired old lady. I even started to
suspect the slow-moving tractor was part of a plot to
keep me from losing my suspected shadows.

I turned left on Eight Mile Road, when the turnoff
for my brother's place wasn't for two more miles. If
the headlights behind me followed, I'd know I was
being tailed. The only thing out this way on Eight Mile
Road was an abandoned farm and a herd of antelope.
Of course, if they had followed me, I'd have led them
to the perfect place to torture and murder me. Unless
a shifter was hanging out with the herd, the antelope
wouldn't be good witnesses if it came time to identify
my killers.

I breathed shallowly to stave off puking as mental
pictures of my untimely demise and the scent of the
Colonel's finest came together in unwelcome combination.

No one followed me, thankfully.

Unfortunately, the detour around the countryside
meant I arrived at my brother's house fifteen minutes
later than I'd promised.

James met me on the steps of his blue-and-white
double-wide trailer. He glowered at me, then at the
bag of chicken and sides I carried. "You're late. And I
thought you were going to make pizza."

My brother's trailer was parked on five acres of mostly barren, rocky land. Any vehicle coming near created such a plume of dust and dirt that they'd be immediately visible. No dust meant no one was near.

"Damn it, Donnie. What the hell is wrong with you?"

I returned my wandering gaze to my brother. "Oh, sorry. Yeah, I ran into a problem at the grocery store, then there wasn't time. So, chicken."

"Janey!" James bellowed through the open screen door. "Let's go. We're going to be late."

For the first time, I noticed James's outfit. Not the typical beat-up jeans and T-shirt he wore when he wasn't working. Tonight he had on jeans that were so new they appeared stiff and a button-down, western-style shirt. Wow. When he said date night, he meant the real deal. I didn't think about it very often, but sometimes the resemblance between my brothers, especially James and me, hit me. Looking at James all cleaned up was like looking into a mirror of myself in ten years.

I met Janey in the middle of the living room. "Thanks for doing this." She smiled up at me, and I couldn't help but smile back. She was a little thing, barely five feet tall, but she kept my blustering brother and her quartet of sons in line better than any Army general could. And she did it with a sweet smile and soft voice.

"Not a problem. You know I enjoy hanging with the little hellions."

"That's because you're the same mental age as them," James muttered. He beckoned Janey toward the door.

I refused to let him see how the words twisted me up inside. I smirked, then flipped him off. I bent down to press a quick kiss to Janey's cheek. "By the way, congrats,

Mama." I set the bag of food on the long table. "Boys! Time to eat!"

Four pairs of feet came thundering down the narrow hall from their bedrooms.

"Get out of here," I told my brother. "Have fun. Go wild. Be crazy. I've got things under control."

He grabbed the keys off the rack by the door. "We'll be back by eleven." He turned to the boys. "Be good."

My nephews descended on the buckets of chicken and sides like a pack of starving, well, coyotes. I tried not to think about Mafia Hit Man while they ate. I was so busy trying not to worry about William and the trouble he was probably in that I forgot to feed myself. By the time I remembered that food was a good thing, there was nothing left on the table but chicken bones and biscuit crumbs. They'd even finished off the coleslaw, and that was cabbage. A vegetable.

One hour and a dozen video games later, I had them settled in front of the TV watching an animated movie, and I was raiding the kitchen. I pulled out bags of flour and sugar, some eggs, butter, and a canister of cocoa powder. Before I knew it, four little boys had joined me. They sifted flour, measured ingredients, and made one hell of a mess.

"Whatcha think, Uncle Donnie?" Jeremy, the youngest, looked up from the chocolate cupcake he was decorating with blue frosting. There was as much blue on his face, shirt, and hands as there was on the cake. Jeremy was a cutie. Actually, the poor kid reminded me so much of myself at that age. He had the same curiosity, the same inquisitiveness. I doubted he'd be one to fall into line with family expectations as easily as his older brothers would. I made a promise to myself that he'd have an ally, something I didn't have, if he decided to strike out on his own path in life.

"It's perfect." I cringed at the thought of the cleanup that would be required, but the smile he gave me made it totally worth it. "Tommy Granger," I snapped without looking away from my own chocolate masterpiece, "if you eat one more spoonful of frosting, you'll have to run laps around the property. Your father will kill me if he comes home and you're all hopped up on sugar."

I heard the spoon drop back into the frosting bowl. "Good boy."

"How does he always know?" Brad, the second youngest, asked.

"He has eyes in the back of his head, just like Mama."

I kept my smile to myself. I wasn't going to tell them that fifteen years ago it would have been me eating frosting from the bowl. Or that the toaster on the counter was perfectly positioned to catch the reflection of little boys at the table. No need to give away all my secrets.

I thought I saw a shadow pass by the kitchen window. I stilled, concentrating to hear any out-of-place noises outside. There was nothing. No rumble of a car engine, no sound of footsteps on the porch.

No chirrups of the crickets.

I set down the sandwich bag I'd been using to squeeze frosting onto a cupcake.

"Where are you going?" Jeremy asked when I stood, then walked to the trailer's front door.

"Just checking on something." I paused by the door, listening carefully. Still too quiet. I eased the door open and peered out.

At first I didn't see it. I didn't notice anything out of place. Then I looked down. There, on the welcome mat Janey had put out after the snow melted, sat a shucked ear of corn.

"Son of a bitch." I covered my mouth with my hand. This wasn't good. Not good at all.

Chapter Seven

I RUSHED to my car the second James and Janey returned. Breaking the law, I dialed Ford on my cell phone while I sped down the highway back into town. When the call connected, I demanded "I need William's phone number" before Ford could utter "hello."

There was a pause. "Why are you telling me this?"

"You work at the college. You can get his contact information."

Another long pause. "Donnie, I work in the biology department. As a TA. I don't really have access to a professor in the social sciences department. I guess I could get you his office number."

"What good would that do me? He's not going to be in his office this late on a Friday night."

Ford sighed. I could hear the jangle of change as the café's register drawer slammed shut. Ford always used more force than necessary. "This isn't a good time. Buddy's is packed. I can do some digging tomorrow to see if I can turn anything up."

"I can't wait that long."

"Don't be melodramatic. Just because you've got a thing for—"

I didn't have time for this. "My family is in danger."

There was a long pause, in which all I heard was the distant murmur of conversation in the background. Then Ford sighed. "Fine. I'll get someone to cover me at Buddy's, and I'll see what I can find out for you."

I disconnected the call. It was a miracle I didn't run into anyone or anything as I drove to the apartment I shared with Ford. My brain was so full of fear and anger, there was no room for mundane details like intersections and road signs.

I burst through the door to find Ford on the couch, his computer glowing on the coffee table in front of him. "Well?" I demanded.

He glowered up at me from beneath dark brows. "I've made a few calls. I should hear something soon."

"Damn it." I slammed the door behind me and stalked across the room to loom over him. "I need to find him."

Ford pushed his computer back and propped his feet on the coffee table. "Why don't you go see him? You know where he lives, right?"

"I can't. I'm being followed. I told them I don't know who he is or where to find them. They'll catch on pretty quick if I show up at his house."

Ford shot up straight. "What do you mean, you're being followed? What the hell is going on?"

"I don't know," I wailed, throwing up my hands. It was a melodramatic gesture, but I was feeling a hair melodramatic. Terror could do that to a guy. "Mafia Hit Man cornered me in the vegetables, then he molested an ear of corn, and he showed up while we frosted cupcakes. I don't know what to do, but I'm completely freaked-out and I don't know what to do about it."

Ford held up a hand. "Stop. Just... stop. A mafia hit man molested an ear of corn and then frosted cupcakes?"

I plopped down next to him on the couch, took a deep breath, then tried again. I explained about Mafia Hit Man and the scene at the produce section. Then about the corn on Janey's welcome mat.

"And all of this has something to do with William?" I couldn't tell if it was skepticism or concern in Ford's voice. Sometime during my story, he'd planted his feet back on the floor so he could lean forward with his elbows braced on his knees.

"Yeah. They want him, and to get him, they think they need me. To get me, they threatened my family. What could he have possibly done to earn a couple of creeps on his tail?"

"I don't think it matters." Ford closed his laptop. He usually seemed pretty serious, but just now his expression was downright grim. "You don't need his phone number, Donnie. You need to call the police and stay as far away from him as you can. Don't look for him. Don't talk to him. You need to drop off of these freaks' radar before you get hurt."

"I can't do that. What if they find him and I could have warned him?"

"What if they do more to your family than leaving a corncob on the porch?" he countered.

He had a point. "Look, I just need to find out what he's gotten me involved in and what I need to do to protect my family. Once that's done, I'm out of it. Really."

No hiding the skepticism in the look he shot me.

"Really." I mentally crossed my fingers. What if William needed my help? Granted, he didn't act like he needed my help. And the whole security setup at his place made it look like he could handle things without my help. But what did I know about it? Superheroes had sidekicks for a reason, right?

Ford's phone rang, interrupting the hard stare he was giving me. I held my breath and leaned closer while he answered the call. Ford, the bastard, turned the other direction. He grunted and grabbed a pencil and scrawled some numbers on an old pizza receipt. I grabbed the slip of paper and darted to my bedroom even as I started to dial.

The phone only rang once before the call connected and William's deep voice came through the line. "Donnie?"

At first I was taken aback. How had he known it was me? Then I remembered he was some kind of superhero/superspy guy, so he probably had all sorts of gadgets to tell him stuff like who was calling. Then I also remembered most phones have caller ID, so all he had to do was see *Donald Granger* flash on his screen.

"What have you gotten me into?" I crawled onto my bed with my back against the headboard. "One of those freaks accosted me at the grocery store, and I may never eat corn again. And I used to like corn. Especially corn on the cob. Grilled."

"What happened?"

I was kind of glad he'd stopped me. Now really wasn't the time to get into a corn-cooking tutorial. I cleared my throat. It was always harder to keep a rein on my mouth when anxiety hijacked my brain. "One of those goons found me, demanded I spill all I know about you, then followed me to *my brother's house*, while I was babysitting *my nephews*, and left a threat for me to find."

"What kind of threat? A note?"

"Not a note." I wish it had been a note. Visions of Mafia Hit Man's hands snapping the cob in half after stroking it were enough to make my blood run cold. Really, I might never be able to eat corn again. "A corncob."

"A corncob?"

"Don't give me that look," I demanded.

"We're on the phone."

"Doesn't matter. I can practically see the look you're giving me. The one that says Donnie, the silly coyote, has lost his marbles. Or is making some lame attempt to see you again. Or something. You think I'm being ridiculous."

"Tell me about the corncob."

I let out an exasperated huff of air. "Fine." I gave him the details. Every time I told the story, the corn thing got creepier and creepier. I was beginning to think Mafia Hit Man had an unnatural obsession with phallic vegetables. I'd have hated to see what he'd do to a cucumber, or worse, asparagus.

"I'll be there in ten minutes." The growl in William's voice sounded more bearlike than buffalo-like.

"What? No!" I surged off my bed. "They're watching me. If you come here, they'll find you. And give them more reason to threaten my family."

"They'll never see me." His voice gentled. "I will make sure your family is protected. I promise. It will be safer for you and them to get you out of the way."

"But—"

"I'll be there in ten. Pack a bag."

"A bag? What—" He hung up on me. Damn it. Now what was I supposed to do? I glared at my silent phone. I guess I was going to pack a bag.

"COME with me."

I yipped, and the glass of water I'd been sipping from slipped from my hand. I hadn't heard a knock or a door opening or anything, but there William stood, barely two feet away from me. His hand darted out, grabbing the glass before it could hit the floor. Man, the dude was fast. And quiet. And in my kitchen. "How the hell did you get in here?"

"Patio door."

"But… but…." I bit back my stutters, cleared my throat, then tried again. "We're on the third floor."

He shrugged. Just shrugged, like three stories was nothing.

"I thought you were a bison, and last I checked, buffalo don't have wings." Then I remembered the wrought iron stairs leading from the patio to the parking lot. Jesus, sometimes I was a dumbass.

"Where's your stuff?"

I jerked my head toward the living room. Without a word, he crossed the space from kitchen to living room—a whopping six steps—and grabbed the duffel bag I'd stashed on the couch.

Ford came out of his room and into the hall. He crossed his arms over his chest. "I still don't think this is a good idea. What do you know about him?"

"We've been through this," I said with a quick glance at William. And we had. We'd spent the whole time I was throwing clothes into a bag with Ford telling me all the reasons running into hiding with a virtual stranger was a bad idea. And, to his credit, he had a point. But I didn't know what else I could do to protect my family. I truly believed William, with his secret agent home security system, probably had the skills needed to keep me and my family safe. Wishful thinking, maybe, but what else could I do? Go to the cops and tell them some dude with an attitude threatened me with a corncob? As far as I knew, mutilating produce wasn't a crime.

Ford turned to William, shoulders rounded. "I don't trust you."

William shrugged. "You don't need to."

Ford wasn't intimidated by William's curt answer. He stepped closer, invading William's personal space. I was surprised to see they were the same height. Somehow William always seemed bigger to me. "If anything happens to Donnie, anything at all, I'll hold you personally responsible." A hint of violence, something I wasn't used to with Ford, edged his voice.

"No one will hurt him while he's with me."

This was too much. "Excuse me? I am in the room, you know. Also, I'm not a little kid." I glared at my roommate.

They both ignored me. Damn alpha men.

"I'm not worried about other people hurting him," Ford said. "I'm worried about you hurting him."

Okay, that was beyond enough. I flung out a hand to halt Ford. "You know what? Back off. I'm a grownass adult. I can take care of myself."

"Yeah, but you're not the one who'll have to deal with an entire pack of coyotes when you disappear from the face of the earth. I want to hear from you at least once a day while you're gone. If I don't, I'm calling the sheriff."

William just stood there, damn near placid, as if an angry bird of prey wasn't threatening him.

"Fine. Whatever." I grabbed the sleeve of William's flannel shirt and dragged him to the door. He ruined my dramatic exit by stopping dead in the middle of the room. I almost fell at the abrupt change in momentum. I scowled up at him. "What now?"

"Patio."

"Seriously?"

At his implacable look, I sighed and changed directions, tugging him to the kitchen. "Don't you think this is taking things a little too far?"

"No."

I huffed. "Why not?"

"They have someone watching the front of your building."

It was my turn to stop. "What?"

"They have someone watching your building."

"Yeah, I heard you the first time. I just can't believe it."

"You knew they were watching you." William placed his hand between my shoulder blades and encouraged me—with a pretty hard shove, thank you very much—to keep moving.

"I thought maybe they were keeping tabs on me or asking around. Not actually setting up some kind of surveillance op." Two steps later, I stopped again. "Wait! Is Ford safe? What if they come after him?"

"They don't have any reason to go after him."

"But why do they want to go after me? I mean, we barely know each other. Why do they think I'd know how to find you? So I stared at you a few times. It's not like we were ever seen together." I thought by this time I was talking to myself. Maybe babbling. Either way,

William didn't respond, and I probably didn't want him to. My crush was bad enough. I didn't really need him clued in. At least no more than he already was. Stupid lack of subtlety.

Even with our starting and stopping, we'd managed to cover the six steps back into the kitchen. All William had to do was reach out and slide the patio door open. He pressed a finger over his lips in the universal signal to shut it and peeked out. Looking both ways, he gestured me to follow him. "Quietly," he murmured.

I rolled my eyes. I was a coyote shifter. We were all about quiet. We could sneak up on a rabbit without making a sound. With my first step, I ran into Ford's bike and watched with dread as it started to topple forward. William caught it, sending me an admonishing look even as he settled it back on its kickstand.

Yep. Sneaky. That was me.

Thankfully, the rest of the trip down the wrought iron stairs and into the parking lot was made with a lot less action. The danger of the situation struck me as my feet hit the blacktop. I was actually sneaking out of my apartment to hide from guys threatening my family. I was trusting someone I barely knew to protect the people who meant the most to me. The panic I'd felt on the ride from my brother's house surged back, and it was all I could do to keep my breathing even. I don't think I blinked as we weaved through the vehicles in the lot. William didn't turn onto the sidewalk or walk to any of the cars parked on the street. Instead he led me through the abandoned field that sat adjacent to the parking lot. It was a great place for chasing squirrels but didn't offer anything in the way of protection from prying eyes.

With every cricket's buzz and every slamming door down the street, my heart pounded. I kept my eyes trained on the back of William's head, shadowing his every movement. It seemed to help my nerves. It also kept me from noticing anything else around us. When we stopped, it took a moment for me to snap into our surroundings. He'd halted in front of a newer crossover vehicle, something rated for low emissions. I wasn't sure what I'd expected, but not that. Maybe something as burly and manly as he was?

William escorted me to the passenger-side door. I climbed in, and while he walked the distance around the hood to the driver's side, I examined the interior. Like his home, the car lacked a certain amount of personality. There wasn't even a pine-tree deodorizer hanging from the rearview mirror. No empty soda bottles, no fast-food bags like you'd find in my car. Unlike his home, the car wasn't decked out in superspy technology. I poked at the radio in case it had a missile launcher or something similar. Nope. Just a radio. Tuned to National Public Radio, of all things.

"Your car matches the professor," I said when he opened the door and slid into his seat.

He did one of those single eyebrow lifts, a sort of facial question mark.

I gestured to the dash. "Yeah, you know, practical, socially conscious, a little liberal. What kind of car does the superspy drive?"

He grunted. "This one."

"I gotta admit, that's a little disappointing."

He started the engine before glancing my way. "What does a part-time barista drive?"

"A cheap piece of rusting junk held together by zip ties and duct tape. It gets horrible mileage, but it's got personality to spare."

I refused to let the concerned furrows in his brow, which were highlighted in the blue light from the dash, shame me. It might not be the prettiest car in the area, but at least I wasn't driving around in a soccer-mom vehicle. "So where are we going? Not your place, I assume."

"I'm borrowing a cabin on the outskirts of Yellowstone from a friend."

"Are you going to finally tell me what all this is about? I mean, why are these creepy dudes from the city trying so hard to find you? Who are they? Now they know where you work, where you live. How come they haven't gotten you yet?"

William sighed but kept his eyes trained on the road. "I'll explain everything when we get to the cabin."

"Why can't you explain now? I'm here. You're here. There's no one around to overhear." I let the words I'd just said run through my mind a couple of times. The last three sentences could totally be said in the "I scream, you scream, we all scream for ice cream" cadence. And then, since exploring my inner poet wasn't going to get me anywhere, I dragged my mind back to the conversation at hand. Or at least to the conversation I wanted at hand. "Damn it, William. At least tell me my family will be safe. I mean, if I disappear, what's to stop them from following through on their threat?"

"Your family will be fine. I've taken care of it. You have to trust me on that."

"Trust you? I barely know you. I'm already trusting you more than I probably should just by sitting in this car with you, driving to God knows where. For all I know, you're some kind of serial killer planning on dispatching me in the woods for the bears to eat. Or you're taking me to a sadistic dungeon where you're going to do all sorts of depraved things to me."

If I hadn't been watching him so closely, I probably wouldn't have noticed the way his lips quirked. That little movement caused heat to slide from my chest to my groin. Especially when I imagined the kinky, depraved things he could do to me in some secret dungeon in the woods. I cleared my throat. Seriously, that wasn't my scene. But it might be fun to play a little.

I pinched my thigh. *Back on track, Donnie.* "You promise they're safe?"

He nodded.

"You know," I said, exasperation sharpening my voice, "I can appreciate the strong, silent thing, but it does get a little old. If you don't want to have the important conversation, can we at least talk about something? The silence and the whole creepy-city-dudes-following-me thing is starting to make me edgy. The least you can do is help distract me. I mean, I'm going to be a jittery mess in a few minutes."

"I'm driving."

"So? You afraid you're going to hit a deer or something?"

"No, I'm watching for tails."

I held my hand to my suddenly queasy stomach. There was a thought.

Over the next several miles, I watched the side mirror obsessively and spun around in my seat to glance behind us, looking for headlights. I didn't see any, but William didn't seem to relax as we opened up more distance between us and Cody.

Staying quiet was never something I did well. It didn't take long for my mouth to go into avalanche

mode. A defense mechanism to keep me from totally
freaking out. "You know, a buddy of mine used to work
out this way. County road crew. He hooked me up with
a job the summer after high school. The money was
pretty good, but the work sucked. I was one of those
guys who held signs that said Slow or Stop. For ten
hours a day, I baked in the sun, getting windburned and
sunburned. I had to wear a hard hat and one of those
neon orange vests. I considered quitting, but then I'd
have had to admit to my dad that I couldn't cut it. He'd
tried to get me a job with the oil company, working
with him and my brothers, but no way was I doing that.
So I dealt with the sore feet and god-awful hours. I was
never so glad for school to start as I was then."

"Why didn't you want to work with your family?"

I practically jumped at William's question. I hadn't
been convinced he'd actually been listening to me
ramble. "Oh, uh, well, *everyone* in my family works for
the oil company. And I just couldn't see myself doing
it, you know? Don't get me wrong, it's a good job, but I
was the first in my family to go to college, so it seemed
like I should be doing something else. So I ended up
roasting on the roadside for three months."

"What was your major?"

Wow, look at us. Having an actual conversation.
I felt a little bad about it, but he was stonewalling me,
so I asked. "Are you actually interested in my answers,
or are you just keeping me occupied so I don't ask any
more important questions? Distracting me, like with
the sex that night."

"Of course I'm interested." He didn't even pause
when he answered, sounding sincere and a little hurt
that I'd even question it. "Sending you away, ending

things before they could go any further, was about protecting you, not disinterest."

Funny. I trusted him to keep my family and Ford safe, but I didn't trust him to tell me the truth about that. It was all sorts of messed up.

"So, your major?" he prompted.

"Undeclared. It wasn't that I was going after something in particular. I just knew there was more to life than oil fields, and college seemed the way to go. It took me two years to realize that college wasn't going to be the answer."

"So you went to work at Buddy's. Was that your answer?"

"Oh, I didn't land at Buddy's right away. First I ended up at Dale's Bootery, but it didn't take long for me to realize cowboy boots and saddles weren't my thing. I worked with Billy Bickle doing landscaping, and that was fun for a while, but then winter came, so I had to find something else. I landed at Buddy's about a year and a half ago, and it seems to be sticking."

"How many jobs have you had?"

If I thought his face had been unexpressive before, he seemed neutral as a statue now. I started counting off on my fingers. "Road crew, sales clerk. Landscaper, then gas station. Ugh, I'll never do that again. I only worked at the hotel for a week, so I don't think that should count." I kept ticking away. "I guess about eight? There were a few random ones too, but those were mostly to help out friends and family. Like the time I helped haul hay one weekend."

"So that's, what, eight jobs since high school?"

If I'd been in my coyote form, my hackles would have risen at the censure in his voice. "You know what?

I get enough disapproval from my father about my work history. I don't need it from you."

He didn't say anything to that, but I thought I saw his jaw clenching. Good. I hoped he got TMJ. I angled myself away from him until I was mostly facing the passenger-side window. I don't know why I was so upset. Well, I kind of did. It would have been nice if there was someone in my life who didn't judge me. First my family. Now William. Even my friends, like Ford, couldn't help asking when I was going to settle down with a real job or go back to school. What was wrong with what I was doing? I was happy. Nobody was hurt. What was the harm?

Chapter Eight

FORTY minutes later, we drove along a dirt road leading deeper and deeper into the forest. Anyone without a shifter's innate night vision would have been totally lost. Even I didn't see where the narrow path—calling it a road was really stretching the truth—led. William stopped his oh-so-practical car in a small clearing, and it took me a moment to realize we'd arrived. The cabin, as he'd called it, was set back behind a veritable wall of trees, nearly invisible even under the harsh glare of the headlights. And what I saw... well, let's just say it was unlike any cabin I'd ever seen. The house was huge, a fascinating combination of rustic, natural logs, and modern architecture. I was pretty sure the thing was bigger than my whole apartment building.

"You call this a cabin?"

William shut off the ignition and pocketed the keys. "What else?" He slid out of the car and grabbed a duffel bag from the back seat. I got out, grabbed my own bag, and followed him up the wide wooden porch and into the house. The foyer—yes, the "cabin" had a foyer, complete with brass-accented tables and a huge winding staircase leading to the upper floor—stretched out in front of us, ending at a huge stone fireplace.

"Pick a room upstairs."

"Which room is yours?" Though I hadn't meant it suggestively, the question hung heavy in the air between us. "So I know which one to avoid," I added quickly, which only made things worse. A little too vehement.

"I'm at the end of the hall, on the right. You should hit the sack. It's been a long night, and you need some sleep."

"Oh hell no." I dropped my bag and stalked up to William. "You need to stop treating me like a child."

"I'm not treating you like a child."

"Oh yeah? You're sending me to bed. Unless it's an invitation for wild monkey sex, it's treating me like a child."

"Donnie...."

"You said we'd talk, and you're not driving anymore, so you will talk. I deserve some explanations."

He turned away.

I grabbed his arm. "I'm getting sick and tired of you putting me off. I refuse to let you distract me with inane orders or stupid questions. So, speak."

He spun quicker than I gave him credit for. "It isn't as easy as all that," he snapped. "It's going to change the way you look at me. I'm not sure I'm ready for that."

I took an involuntary step backward. "What do you mean?"

He shook his shaggy head. "Never mind. I'm going to start a fire. It gets cold at night." William tossed his own bag on the foot of the stairs and continued to a wooden chest that turned out to hold firewood. "Then I'll explain what I can."

He hauled a couple of large hunks of wood out of the box and set them in the fireplace as though the fate of the world rested on their exact placement. "I can't tell you everything." Before I could snap at him about putting me off again, he continued. "Some of it is classified."

On either side of the fireplace was a small alcove, each one holding a tan love seat and a reading chair. I scooted into one of the chairs and tucked my legs up. It was about time I got some answers. When he didn't look like he was going to go on, I waved at him. "Continue."

William added skinny sticks and a couple of sheets of rolled newspaper to the bundle in the fireplace. When everything was placed just so, he grabbed a long matchstick from a tall silver cylinder near the hanging iron fire tools. "The men who have been looking for me, and who are following you, are part of an international weapons-trafficking syndicate." He flicked the match and stared at the resulting flame for a second.

I fell back into the tan seat. "They're what now?"

"The organization they belong to was recently brought down through a combined effort by several national and international organizations. Those individuals who were not arrested are attempting to get revenge on those they hold responsible." William spoke in an even, matter-of-fact way that sounded as though he were reading a report.

"But why do they want you? You're a college professor."

He touched the burning match to the newspaper tucked into the wood. The paper burst into flame, illuminating his face with an orange glow. It was a stoic, almost scary look.

"You are a college professor, aren't you?"

William tossed the match in the flames and stood. "Yes, I'm a college professor. Now."

My breath caught in my throat. "Now? Which means before...."

He settled onto the love seat, crossing one leg over the opposite knee. The position was meant to look relaxed, but I didn't buy it. When he spoke it was in the neutral, straightforward way I assumed he used when lecturing students. "For the last five years, I've worked undercover to infiltrate the weapons-trafficking organization."

I nearly fell out of my seat. "Say again?"

"I worked protection detail for Marc Conrad, the head of the organization."

I glanced at his broad chest and tightly muscled arms. Yeah, I could totally see him pulling that off. But.... "Why you? I assume the degree is legit. So what does a professor of political science know about... about undercover missions and such? I mean, did they recruit you in college or something? And who exactly is *they*? Who sent you on this assignment?"

"I was recruited in college, actually. In a roundabout way. I won't divulge the organization—national and international security. I was approached while interning in Washington, DC, the summer before my senior year. I came from money, I spoke a few languages. I was just the kind of guy they were looking for. The senator I worked for had contacts. They provided specialized training, and for the next five years I was brought in on smaller missions while I worked on my masters and PhD."

"But… but…." My head was spinning. I had no idea what to make of this. I'd have thought it was all some tall tale, something he dug out to impress people, if I hadn't seen his version of home security. Surely only someone with the experience, know-how, and contacts would set up such an impenetrable system. Or a truly deluded, paranoid, independently wealthy person. I examined William. I didn't *think* he'd ever displayed any paranoid tendencies. Sure, there was the *Mission: Impossible* dash from my apartment to his car. On the other hand, I was the one who figured out the bad guys weren't who, or what, they seemed.

I cleared my throat. "And why are the creepy dudes after you? You said the weapons-trafficking organization had been brought down."

"We cut the head off—"

I let out a choking gasp. "You cut off someone's head?"

"We cut the head off *the organization* by taking down the top tier of leadership. Typically, the organization will fall apart after something like that. Or they lie low for a few years and regroup."

"These guys didn't?"

"After those men showed up in Cody, I made a few calls. Conrad's son, Robert, who had appeared to take no interest in his father's enterprise, stepped into the leadership role and started rebuilding the organization. Rumor has it his top priority is exacting revenge on those responsible for his father's arrest."

"Meaning you."

"And others. But, yeah, me in particular."

"Why you in particular?"

William leaned forward, bracing his elbows on his knees. "Being undercover… sometimes you have do things you're not proud of, for the good of the mission."

"Lie, cheat, kill?" I suggested.

He nodded. "It might have been easier if that were all I'd done. After a couple of years, Conrad actually *cared* about me. I was invited to family events, not as hired muscle, but as a friend of the family. As family. I think that's the betrayal—the way I'd betrayed his father—Robert can't get past. That's why he's so determined to make me pay."

"How did they find you? I know you weren't dumb enough to use your real name or anything." I might be a college dropout, but even I could see the idiocy in such a move. And William wasn't an idiot.

"Of course not." William's mouth pursed into a thin line. "I don't know how they discovered me or my location. That is the next item on my agenda. There were very few individuals who knew my connection. Even fewer who knew my real name. I wasn't officially on any government agency's payroll. It had to be someone on the inside, someone I trusted."

"How are you going to find out who it is?"

His eyes narrowed, the intensity in them causing little shivers to run through me. "As soon as I can get my hands on one of the guys after me, I'll ask him." Was there anything sexier than a man on a mission?

"You think it will be that easy?" *No sexy thoughts. No sexy thoughts.* I let the mantra run through my head, hoping it would keep the sexy thoughts at bay. No way was I going to get trapped in that... *trap*... again. No distractions. I had more important things—like the safety of my family and Ford—to worry about. My stupid crush on this man had already caused too many problems. And he'd made it clear the other morning that our night together had been just that: a distraction. Besides, international weapons traffickers running amok in Cody were enough to worry about.

"For a couple of men who should be completely out of place around here, I haven't had any luck finding their base."

"You mean where they're staying?"

He nodded.

"You've checked the local hotels and motels?"

"I've tried. So far, everyone has been unwilling to share guest information without a warrant, something I don't have. Privacy issues. There are analysts I've worked with in the past who could run a simple search and let me know within minutes if these guys are registered anywhere, even if they faked their identities, but I don't know who I can trust. I'm waiting to hear from an old contact, one unconnected to the bust, to see if they can run the search."

"I can call the Marriott. Jesse's still the manager there. I'm sure he'll tell me if I ask." If I asked really nicely and maybe flirted a little. Jesse and I had dated briefly, and he'd made some comments lately hinting that he'd like to try again. I'd been avoiding him, but I could deal if it helped get the freaks out of town and away from my family. *And from William*, a little voice in my head added. To which I responded *Shut up. He's a big boy and can take care of himself.* To which the voice teased *But you want to keep him safe because you* liiike *him*. I mentally scowled at the stupid voice. *Shut it.*

William stared at me, head cocked to the side, which pulled me out of the ridiculous internal argument. Seriously, who did that? And for the record, that little voice was a whiny bitch.

"No." Just one word, spoken like he expected it to be obeyed without question. Surely he knew by now I questioned everything.

"But why not? It would just take a phone call. I bet I know people at some of the other hotels too. I could have some answers, or at least narrow down your list, within an hour or two."

"No. I can't risk word getting out. You stay out of it."

"But I'm already in it." I waved my arm around to encompass the mansion-masquerading-as-a-cabin. "Otherwise I wouldn't be here."

"I've got some feelers out. I don't need you tangling yourself into things too."

If he hadn't said that as if he were telling a little kid he was too young to play with the grown-ups, I probably wouldn't have reacted the way I did. Probably. I may not have been the adultiest adult in the room, but that didn't make me irresponsible. It didn't make me a child.

I pushed myself out of the chair and stalked toward him. "You've got to stop doing that."

He raised an eyebrow. Oh no. That stupid eyebrow meant to make me feel inferior. Well, screw that.

"You've got to stop treating me like some dumb kid who's in your way." I tugged my shirt off and flung it at his feet. "Do I look like a kid?"

I took a little pleasure—okay, a lot of pleasure—in the heat blooming in his eyes. I clenched my abs to show off their definition. I wasn't built, not like he was, but I'd work with what I had. While his gaze stayed locked about belly button level, I traced the dusting of hair that disappeared under the waistband of my jeans.

It was kind of hot, watching him watch me. William may not have taken me seriously a lot of the time, but there was no denying he wanted me.

"What are you doing?"

I braced my hands on his shoulders and straddled his lap. "What does it look like I'm doing?"

He settled back, making room for me, his hands resting at my hips.

I made a production out of getting into just the right spot, ensuring I rubbed against the growing bulge beneath his zipper. His fingers tightened at my waist.

"Tell me"—I leaned forward and nipped his ear—"are you thinking of me like a kid now?"

He bucked gently under me, grinding his denim-covered cock against my ass. "I've never thought of you like a kid," he growled.

I released his shoulders to dig my hands into his thick hair. "Prove it."

Oh holy fuck, he did. In a single smooth motion, William surged out of the chair, me still clutched against his body, and hauled me the two steps to the rug in front of the fireplace. He laid me down and draped himself over my prone body. I didn't even have time to gasp before his mouth was on mine in a mind-altering, alpha-dominating kiss. The warmth from the fire bathing the side of my face had nothing on the heat his body generated. The thick nap of the rug, softer than I'd imagined it would be, cushioned my back from the hardwood floor and contrasted with the soft flannel of William's shirt. The combination of textures and the weight of his body on mine had me soaring even before his hands got in on the action.

I forgot the point I'd been trying to make under the almost violent assault to my mouth. His teeth and tongue scattered whatever senses I had left, leaving me lost in pure sensation.

I wanted to touch, to feel his skin under my hands. To taste his skin under my tongue. I also wanted to lay back and bask in the pleasure of his body on mine. I'd never been good at making up my mind between two things I wanted. I didn't want to choose. I wanted to do it all. William reared back, taking the choice away from me. Kneeling above me, he pulled the flannel shirt over his head. I heard a couple of buttons scatter, but my focus stayed on the flesh he revealed.

I dragged my hands up the soft skin of his side. So soft, almost delicate. William twitched and let out a little huff at my tickling fingertips. I decided then and there to make it my life's mission to find and exploit every ticklish spot on his body. I would devote all the hours necessary to make him squirm.

I walked my fingers up the ladder of his ribs, and his huff turned into a choked gasp. I ran the back of my fingernails through the hair at his armpits as he escaped from his flannel. He tossed the shirt aside and caught each of my hands in one of his. "Enough," he growled, and the husky, rumbly sound of it melted me. I sighed and relaxed onto the rug.

William released my hands, propped himself above me, and braced his hands on the floor above my shoulders. I couldn't help the grin that stretched my face. This close—face-to-face—I could see the paler brown flecks in his dark brown eyes. The stern mask he usually wore had gentled, and it made him look several years younger, closer to my age than the midthirties I guessed him to be.

He lowered his body like he was doing a push-up. I was sure he was going to kiss me. He didn't. Instead he brushed his stubbly jaw against my cheek, then nuzzled my neck. The unexpected tenderness of it had me melting even more. Good thing I was made of skin, muscle, and bones. If I looked the way I felt, I'd be a puddle of warm wax with a sappy smile.

William's teeth scraped along my Adam's apple, hard enough to zing little jolts of electricity from there all the way to my toes, and suddenly those muscles that felt like melted wax started to tense. My breath caught. He sucked skin between his teeth, and the pinch of pain made me gasp. It was my turn to squirm.

He pushed himself backward, letting the weight of his upper body press against my hips and thighs. His new location put his head in line with my pecs, and he wasted no time trying that whole teeth-scraping thing on first one nipple, then the other. And, holy shit, I had no idea the teeth-scraping thing would feel that fricking fantastic.

My body wanted to arch up into the caress, but his weight kept me still, which seemed to exacerbate the impact. It was frustrating and exhilarating at the same time. My hands were free to roam, though, so I took advantage, burying my fingers into the dark, silky curls of his hair. When William's teeth once again scraped over a nipple, my fingers clenched into fists, pulling at his hair.

I bent my head forward so I could watch him, only to find him looking up at me with an intensity that made the air seize in my lungs. When our eyes met, he very deliberately licked up the mound of my pec, over the sensitized nub of my nipple, and all the way up to my throat. One long, lingering lick. "Christ." I bit my lip to keep from begging him for more, for harder, for something.

Somewhere along the way I'd forgotten about the point I was trying to make. I'm sure it was a very valid point. But the purpose of it got lost somewhere between the clothes coming off and his tongue on my skin. My hands pressed against his shoulders. I don't know if I was trying to push him lower or pull him up. Both seemed equally essential.

Luckily it seemed William could read my indecisions and made the choice for me again.

He shimmied farther down, nibbling and scraping the thin trail of hair that started near my navel and arrowed below the waistband of my jeans. My legs were still trapped under his heavier body, which meant wriggle as I would, I couldn't rock my groin against him as much as I'd like. I couldn't even shift enough to ease the pressure of tight denim stretching over my painfully hard dick.

I dug my nails into the thick muscles of his shoulders and back. I probably left painful scratches in his skin, but William didn't react other than to spear his tongue in the indent of my belly button. He eased off me enough to reach down and tuck his fingers into the waistband of my jeans, releasing the metal button. He cupped his hand around the straining zipper, and I was pretty sure the little blood that remained in my head immediately surged south. I swear, I could count my pulse by the throb of my cock against that zipper.

William rolled to his side so he could lower the zipper and tug my pants off. As soon as I'd kicked the jeans away, I tried to pull him to me for a kiss. Instead he trapped my legs again and nuzzled me through my boxers. Even with the thin cotton barrier, the moist heat from his mouth burned through me. I flung my arms out to steady myself in the suddenly quaking world. My hands tore into the rug, and I had a moment to hope it wasn't some kind of expensive heirloom, because claws broke through my fingertips. I hadn't had an involuntary shift since adolescence, and never a partial shift. But even though I now had claws that ripped through the thick rug I lay on, no other part of my body seemed ready to change.

"I don't think… I mean, if you do that… I won't last." It may not have been a complete, or entirely comprehensible, sentence, but I was proud I got the words out at all.

He chuckled, and the vibration of it traveled over my cock and through my balls. "That's the point." He grazed his teeth up my length. Gently, thankfully. As much as I loved his magical teeth, I didn't think I'd enjoy a sharper application just there. On the other hand, I was pretty sure anything he did at this point would only add to the frenzy of need coursing through me. I didn't think I'd ever been this turned on.

I mentally made a list of homemade bread ingredients so I wouldn't go off too soon. It didn't help. Not unless *gah gah gah* were common recipe components, because when William sucked at the wet spot blooming in the fabric of my boxers, *gah gah gah* were the only words—if you could call them words— my brain could manage.

My heaving breaths and gasping whimpers stopped altogether when William peeled back my underwear and swallowed my cock. And that was it. My mind turned to static, my vision turned to blurry, and I couldn't hear anything over the rushing in my ears. He pulled back until only the head remained in the hot cavern of his mouth. His tongue flicked at the underside, a quick one-two-three, before he fell forward, not pausing until my cock hit the back of his throat and his nose brushed my pubes. Holy freaking hell.

One of his hands joined the party, palming and squeezing my balls. Then one of his fingers found the sensitive space between balls and anus and rubbed. I think I babbled some more. There might have been a few "oh my Gods" interspaced with the *gah gah gah*s. I couldn't focus on anything beyond the race toward orgasm. I teetered on the edge, straining to come and fighting to hold off. I wanted more. I couldn't take any more.

For the third time that night, William made the decision for me. He increased the speed and suction of his mouth until the orgasm crashed into me, shattering me into a million little pieces.

When the million little pieces reassembled sometime later and I could actually form polysyllabic words, I looked down the line of my body to find William resting his head on my hip, his hand moving up and down my leg in a long caress. Our eyes met, and he smiled. It was the gentlest, most open expression I'd ever seen on him. And my insides turned to melted wax again.

"Hey," I said, because I was cool like that. Mr. Smooth, that was me. "I think we've established I am not a child." And because I was so smooth, I just had to make the moment awkward.

He stiffened and the cool, neutral mask fell into place. "Clearly."

He levered himself into a sitting position, and I followed his example. Crap. Foot, meet mouth.

"Sorry." I combed my fingers through my hair, not so much because my hair needed straightening but because I needed something to do with my hands. I folded my legs under me, then grabbed my jeans, dumping them over my lap. "I shouldn't have said that."

William stood, and the orange light from the fire painted him in warm colors, highlighting the swells and valleys of his broad, muscular chest. "It's late. I'll see you in the morning."

Without looking at me again, he snagged his shirt off the love seat and strode through a door on the other side of the entranceway. I flopped back down and stared at the ceiling. When had I become such an ass?

Chapter Nine

I COULDN'T sleep. My scattered brain was a kaleidoscope of images ranging from the bloody deaths of my family and friends to the cold look on William's face when he walked away the night before. As soon as the golden light of dawn crept past the curtains the next morning, I headed downstairs to take an inventory of the kitchen. Cooking always had a way of smoothing out my jagged nerves. Hopefully there would be food in the house. Better would be if there was enough of a selection I could make an awesome breakfast. It was the least I could do after my incredibly obnoxious performance the night before.

I tiptoed down the stairs, ears straining for some sign that William was awake. I knew he was in the house—an empty house had a certain feel to it—but there was no sound of movement.

I hadn't explored the kitchen the night before, but like the rest of the place, it did not fit the description of *cabin*. Gleaming hardwood floors. Glossy granite countertops. A six-burner range and a double oven. Everything a discerning chef could want. And for someone like me, who was more used to the cramped space of a cheap apartment, it was the stuff of dreams.

"Here's hoping the food here matches the setup." I started opening cupboards. I should have known a room this nice would have more to offer than a can of pork and beans or chicken noodle soup. The pantry was stocked with everything I could think of. Rice, pasta, flour, potatoes, sugar, coffee. There were three different flavors of jam, pure maple syrup, and peanut butter. There were even fresh herbs growing on the windowsill. The refrigerator was fully stocked with milk, eggs, butter, and every conceivable condiment. The freezer was overflowing with an assortment of different meats, including steaks, thick-cut bacon, and a package of shrimp. Not to mention chicken, pork chops, and ground beef. I could practically hear the "Hallelujah Chorus" in the background. This was a chef's heaven.

I shut the freezer before I started to gather ingredients for blueberry pancakes and scrambled eggs. William was a vegetarian, so I wouldn't waste my time frying up bacon or sausage. And if he didn't like eggs, then I'd eat them all.

Twenty minutes later, when I was ladling the first scoop of pancake batter onto the griddle, William shuffled into the kitchen. I waved him to the table, then poured him a cup of coffee. I didn't bother with cream or sugar because I knew he preferred his java black. My own cup of joe had enough sweetener to give a bear a toothache.

He watched me with unblinking eyes. He didn't look mad, but just in case…. "I hope you don't mind that I made myself at home in your kitchen."

He grunted and took the cup I offered.

All righty, then. "Look, I shouldn't have presumed. I couldn't sleep, and—"

He stopped my apologies with a wave of his hand. "It's fine. Make yourself at home." He took a long draw from his coffee. "I'm not much of a morning person."

With two mornings to judge this by, I figured he was correct. I cleared my throat. "Right. Well, I have eggs keeping warm in the oven, and the pancakes will be ready in a few. You just"—I gestured vaguely at him—"drink your coffee or whatever."

I reached over to place the salt and pepper shakers on the table and managed to knock them both over. The ceramic set clattered and rolled, spilling granules of salt and flakes of ground pepper all over the surface. "Crap!" Usually I was kind of in my element in front of a stove or oven, but my memories of the previous night, and that night at his house a few days ago, and, well, everything, ensured awkward was the best I could hope for.

"Thanks," William said gruffly when I set a plate piled high with blueberry pancakes and a mound of scrambled eggs in front of him.

"I should have asked. Do you eat eggs? Some vegetarians don't."

"Eggs are fine." Then, as if to prove it, he took a bite.

I didn't know his condiment preferences, so I also laid out a jug of pure maple syrup, a plastic bear full of honey, a jar of blackberry jam, and a jar of homemade apple butter. I watched him make his selection as if this one choice would tell me everything I needed to know about him. Good thing pancake toppings weren't the encyclopedia of all things William. He skipped the jars of sweet and/or fruity and kept it simple with a swipe of butter. That was it. Just butter. Thinking back, I should have known. He always eschewed the sweet pastries at Buddy's, sticking with the savory. Maybe pancakes weren't the best choice.

Screw that, I thought, nearly drowning my own pancakes in maple syrup. If he didn't want them, he didn't have to eat them. I'd made them for me, because I needed something to keep my panicking brain occupied, not for him. The sentiment was maybe 80 percent true and didn't stop the pride blossoming in my chest when he plowed through the meal as though he hadn't eaten in a month. I took a bite. Yeah, they were pretty darned good.

When William set his fork down a little while later, I was gratified to see he'd all but licked his plate clean.

"If you're still hungry, I can make some more eggs. Or whip up another batch of batter."

He pushed his plate away. "No, thank you. That was great." Our eyes met, and I almost forgot what we were talking about. His eyes really were incredible. Deep and dark. "Really, thanks." Then he smiled, which made my fingers go numb, so I dropped my fork. 'Cause I was smooth like that.

I scrambled to pick up my fork and managed to knock my coffee cup into my plate, which dumped the last of my eggs onto my lap. Freaking smooth. I closed my eyes, wishing I could rewind the last thirty seconds. A warm hand covered mine, and my eyes sprung open.

William reached across the table and took the fork from my still numb and fumbling hand. "I'll take care of cleaning up."

"Oh no—" I began, cringing at the mess I'd made. I was a good cook, not a neat cook. Unfortunately the two concepts didn't go hand in hand. Speaking of which, my hand was still in William's.

He squeezed. "I've got this. He who cooks doesn't do dishes."

"Family rule?" I asked, caught up in the gentle tilt of his lips. Not a smile, not quite, but something close.

"My rule."

I nodded, licking suddenly dry lips. "Sounds fair."

His hand left mine as he stood and gathered up the dishes. I took a second to settle my jumping nerves. After a couple of minutes watching William handle cleanup, I stood. I couldn't sit and do nothing while he cleared the mess I'd made. Luckily he didn't argue as I wiped down the table and counters while he loaded the dishwasher. We moved together surprisingly well. Not like *that*. Synchronized moves in the bedroom were not the same as synchronized moves out of the bedroom. Though we maneuvered within the same space, we never stumbled into each other or got in each other's way. Even with Ford, after living and working together as long as we have, we'd still manage to run into each other or be forced to duck under an unexpectedly open cupboard or drawer.

With William it felt right, like we'd done the same domestic routine every morning for years.

As natural as things felt, I had to remind myself this was both temporary and born of necessity. We weren't longtime lovers accomplishing a shared task. We were barely even friendly.

"So what's on the agenda for the day?" I hung a damp towel from a drawer handle to let it dry while William wiped down the stovetop.

"I've got calls to make, some people to track down."

"What should I do?"

He turned his head to look at me. "What do you mean?"

I propped my hands on my hips. "I mean, while you're making your calls, what am I supposed to be doing?"

He shrugged. "Relax. Stay out of trouble."

"That's it?" Anger spiked in my voice. Was he serious?

"Sure. Think of it like a vacation."

"So I'm supposed to sit around twiddling my thumbs while you do your secret-agent thing?" I combed my fingers through my hair, glaring at him. "I can't just sit back and wait while you figure this out. They threatened my family. They threatened *me*. I can barely sit still through a movie, let alone binge on Netflix or whatever. Especially when my friends and family are at risk."

He looked around. "There are no televisions here. There are some books on the shelf in the living room."

Wow, dude was seriously missing the point. "Look, I appreciate your help. I really do. But you've got to give me a break here. Even if my family wasn't in danger, and even if some city thug hadn't threatened me, I'd need to stay busy. If I don't have something to do, I'll likely end up climbing the walls. Probably literally. I will maybe last approximately twenty minutes before losing my mind entirely."

"What do you do with your free time normally?"

"What free time? I work. I babysit my nieces and nephews. I take the occasional class. I bake stuff. Sometimes I hunt. Believe it or not, that takes up most of my time. None of that can be done here."

William crossed his arms over his chest. "I'm trying to keep you safe. It's not my job to entertain you."

Oh, for the love of…. "I don't need to be entertained!
I need to be useful. There's no reason I can't help. You
have your calls to make—let me make some of mine.
You tackle the head of your snake, or whatever you want
to call that Conrad dude. Let me find out where Mafia Hit
Man and Balding Blond Guy are staying. I don't know
jack about crime syndicates or whatever, but I know how
to find someone in Cody."

I looked away. I didn't have any illusions about
how much help I'd be in this kind of investigation. I
took a steadying breath, searching for the calm center
of my internal tsunami. "I'm going to be honest with
you, William. I'm scared. I have no fucking idea what's
going on, and if I have to sit and stare at walls for the
next who-knows-how-long, I'm going to explode.
Either let me help or let me leave."

He thought about it for a minute. I could see
the indecision on his face, the struggle. In the end,
though, he didn't back down. "I can't let you do
either. It's too dangerous. I can't risk you getting in
the way, or you get—"

"Stop!" I clenched my fists, ready to pound someone.
Ready to pound him. "I don't know why you think I'm so
damned inept or what gives you the idea that I'm some
kind of fuckup. It's really starting to piss me off. I'm out
of here."

"You can't leave." William's voice was still emotionless,
but there was something in his eyes, in his face, that
reminded me of that moment last night when he turned away.
Frustration? Hurt? "If you're not here, I can't protect you."

I shored up my willpower. I was probably imagining
things, seeing what I wanted to see. "I'll take my chances."

His face tightened, forming little white creases
around his eyes. "If you go running around half-

cocked, I'll need to use the resources I have protecting your family to protect you instead. Is alleviating your boredom worth risking your family?"

"Bastard." I glared at him, my entire body seizing, first at the thought of my family in danger, and second because he assumed this was about my boredom. I couldn't even form the words to express my frustration. I growled and stormed up the stairs to the room I hadn't been able to sleep in.

Chapter Ten

I TOOK a shower. I tried to take a nap. I decided it was as good a chance to practice meditation as any. Nothing worked. I was angry, frustrated, and, more than anything else, afraid. Staying busy had always been a good way for me to keep from obsessing over things. If I kept my brain occupied with some activity or another, I didn't have to think about family pressure, my future, or all the failures of my past. Now, more than ever, I needed the distraction. My family was in danger. Weirdo thugs were spying on my friends. I was being quarantined in some cabin in the woods for my own protection, treated like a dumb adolescent who knew just enough to be dangerous and not enough to stay out of trouble.

I stared up at the wooden beams of the bedroom ceiling, one leg swinging over the edge of the bed. The constant back-and-forth motion rocked the mattress in a way I usually found soothing, but my agitation only made the movements more and more aggressive until the mattress springs squeaked and the headboard bumped against the wall. Now it sounded like I was having energetic sex. *Awesome.*

I so didn't need to think about sex right now. Twice things had gone further than they should have with William, and both times I ended up feeling like crap afterward. Of course, before the crap, things had felt pretty damn amazing.

I jumped from the bed. It had only been thirty minutes, and I was already bouncing off the walls.

The No Service message on my phone mocked me. I needed to talk to someone. Preferably someone who knew and understood me. Someone I could confess my idiotic behavior of the night before to. I needed to have someone check up on my family. Damn it, I needed Ford. But no, my phone was taking a hiatus from the whole phone thing.

I'd thought to avoid William a while longer as I tried to come to terms with my situation. Guess that was a lost cause.

I tracked the scent of William to an office at the back of the cabin. Large windows faced a stunning forest view I almost missed because I was distracted by the sight of four large-screen monitors, enough sleek electronics to support NASA, and William growling into his phone in what sounded like French. Of course William spoke French. Probably all secret spy types spoke French. Unfortunately, because I didn't speak the language, I had no idea what he was saying, but the menacing tone sent chills down my back. If he ever spoke to me in that tone of voice, I'd probably wet myself.

I didn't think I'd made any noise, but the minute I hit the threshold of the room, he reached over and turned off two of the monitors.

I stared at the blank screens, jaw clenched. It didn't take me more than a second to understand. William didn't think I could be trusted. Or he thought I was a child. Or maybe both. "If you don't want a pissed-off bird of prey breathing down your neck, I need to make a call."

William looked at me for a long moment, the somber expression not matching the threatening tone of voice he'd been using. Not taking his eyes from mine, he growled something into the phone and hung up.

"Ford warned you last night. If he doesn't hear from me, or if he thinks there's the slightest chance that I'm in trouble, he'll come after you. I don't care where you worked or how much technology you've got piled up around you, he'll find you. His tracking skills are damned near supernatural."

He reached under his desk, toying with something I couldn't see. Then he nodded at the phone I still held in my hand. "You can make your call now."

I glanced down. Instead of the No Service message, the display showed two bars. It hadn't been the distance from the city keeping me from calling out; he'd had some kind of block engaged. My grip tightened around my phone. My fingertips tingled as though preparing to sprout claws. I sucked in a breath and tried to will back the coyote's need to protect my fracturing emotions. Shards of fury, frustration, and hurt were tearing me up on the inside.

When the room around me changed from color to black and white, I knew my attempt to battle back the shift was failing. My eyes had started to shift. If there'd been a mirror nearby, I would probably see the coyote's eyes staring back at me.

"I'll let you get back to your calls. The sooner this is resolved, the sooner you can be rid of me. And I thought my family was judgmental. They don't understand me, but at least they don't think I'm an incompetent fuckup who can't be trusted." I turned and left the office, William's somber gaze scraping the nerve endings in my back as I went.

I went straight up to the room I'd occupied the night before. It was as close to my own space as anywhere else in the cabin. I plopped down onto the floor in the corner and drew my knees up to my chest. I took a second to center myself before calling Ford.

I barely let him get out a gruff "So you're still alive" before I demanded, "You trust me, right?"

There was a pause. Ford tended to be a bit taciturn, kind of like the stubborn buffalo shifter downstairs. He also tended to think through his words before he said them, a trait I might want to develop at some point. Even though I knew that about him, the lack of immediate reassurance panicked me. "Shit. You don't trust me either. What have I ever done or said that makes people doubt me? I know I can be reckless sometimes, but I don't lie or cheat. I've never betrayed anyone's trust before. Have I?"

"Slow down, Donnie. I needed to find somewhere quieter to talk. Now, what brought this on?"

Everything—including my behavior the night before—came pouring out of me. I managed to omit the details about William's past. Despite what he may have thought about me, I didn't betray confidences. "He won't let me help. My family's at risk, but he expects me to sit around doing nothing. Why does he think I'm so damned useless?"

I finally stopped talking. And waited. For, like, a really long time. I double-checked the screen of my phone. The call hadn't dropped.

Finally Ford asked, "Have you considered he's trying to keep you out of it to protect you?"

I blinked. "What?"

"Donnie, you don't know squat about the kind of men who are apparently after William. And you managed to end up on their radar."

"I was trying to help him!"

"Exactly. And by trying to help him, you put yourself in danger. I have a feeling that's a hard thing for a guy like him to swallow."

Ford made sense—he usually did. But that didn't automatically mean he was right. I bit my lip, trying to wrap my head around this new theory. "So he, what, feels guilty?"

"If I had to guess, I'd say there was more to it than that."

"What do you mean?"

"Think about it. If all he wanted was to keep you safe, he wouldn't have to kidnap you."

"He didn't kidnap—"

Ford ignored my interruption. "He could have found you a bodyguard, or kept you under surveillance like he's doing with your family. But he didn't. He's keeping you close."

"So you think he actually cares about me or something?"

"What do you think?"

I hated it when Ford answered a question with a question. I thought about it for a second, then shook my head. "I don't know. It could just as easily go back to the trust thing. My family doesn't know anything that could be used against him. They don't even know William. It's just as likely, maybe more so, that he wants me close by so there's no chance of me sharing anything I've learned about him."

"It's not entirely impossible," Ford acknowledged.

I rested my head on my bent knees, closing my eyes. "I can't let myself think he's got a personal interest in me. I'm already too invested in him. I don't know how I'd handle it if I believe he feels something for me, only to find out I'm just an obligation."

"Maybe you should find out."

Easy for Ford to say, I thought a couple of minutes later, after the call ended. He'd never put his heart on the line like that or risked being rejected. I'd been rejected enough, in ways small and large, that I didn't look forward to opening myself up to it again.

On the other hand, I couldn't spend another few hours like the last few. My stomach twisted and ached from the roller coaster of emotions I'd ridden today.

It took twenty minutes for me to work up the nerve to beard the lion in his den. Or, you know, approach the buffalo in his office. William still sat behind his desk, though he wasn't growling at someone in French this time. The monitors he'd turned off earlier were now angled in such a way I couldn't see the screen, even if I'd wanted to.

"You can turn the parental controls back on. I'm done with my phone call."

"Donnie...." His voice trailed off, but he sounded tired. Not frustrated or physically tired, but almost sad. "I'm not trying to parent you."

I nearly said something bitter and snarky but bit back the words with a sigh. He wasn't being confrontational, so I could follow his example. I tucked my thumbs into my jeans pockets. "You can see why I might think so, though, yeah?"

He pushed back from the desk, running a hand through his thick hair. "Yes."

I decided to take a chance. "Why?"

"Why?"

"Why do you insist on treating me like a kid who can't be trusted to avoid chasing a ball into a street full of oncoming traffic? I'm not stupid."

"It's not about trust." The rough timbre of his voice kept me from my instinctive need to contradict him.

"Then what is it?"

"You're reckless." He held up a hand, again stopping me from arguing the point. "You jump into things headfirst, without considering the risk."

"I do not!"

He tilted his head, arching an eyebrow. "How long did it take you to decide to follow me after Conrad's men started asking about me?"

"Yeah, but—"

"Did you stop to wonder about the consequences?"

I threw up a hand. "Stop right there. Did I know what the consequences would be? No, I admit it. But you seem to have forgotten that if I hadn't shown up when I did, Mafia Hit Man"—his lips twitched at my name for the dude—"would have found you."

"I can handle myself."

Geez, the arrogance of this man. And I thought the men in my family were obtuse. At least they didn't have a death wish. "You had a plan in place for an assassination attempt in the middle of Shifter U's campus? Or maybe bullets bounce off your chest like Superman?"

He stood and walked around his desk, moving toward me. Where I'd have expected to see frustration or irritation on his face, I saw *warmth*. The expression was almost like his look last night, after he'd sent me into an earth-shattering orgasm, and before I ruined things with my big mouth.

He reached out and cupped my face in his big hand. It was all I could do not to lean into the heat and comfort of it. I was mad at him, damn it.

"It wouldn't have mattered. I would have done anything—*anything*—to keep you from being hurt. Even take a bullet to the chest in the middle of campus."

Oh holy fuck. How could a few words simultaneously send sunshine through my soul and break my heart?

I opened my mouth a couple of times, unsure of how to respond.

He shook his head and crossed his arms over his chest, a protective movement I wasn't sure he even realized he did. "I've got work to do." He turned his broad back to me, returning to his desk.

I stood there for a few seconds, still reeling from his admission. Finally I left him to his work, the need for a distraction even stronger than before. I hoped William liked baked goods.

Chapter Eleven

MY phone rang just as I closed the oven on the last loaf of rosemary-and-thyme bread dough. William must not have disabled it again. A sign of trust? Or maybe he forgot? Ford's name flashed on the display. I wiped my hands on the dish towel tucked through a belt loop on my jeans.

"Hey." I tucked the phone between my shoulder and ear after hitting the Accept icon. "What's up?"

"There's trouble." Worry edged his voice and had my nerves jangling.

"What happened?" I gripped the edge of the granite countertop almost hard enough to crack its solid surface.

Ford's audible inhale told me he was preparing for something major.

"Someone left a note taped to the door." A pause. "It's Jeremy."

"No. No. No. No." Knees weak, I fell back a couple of steps at the idea of something happening to my nephew.

"Note says he's okay," Ford rushed to assure me. I barely heard him over the dramatic pounding of my heart. "But they want to talk to you."

"Where? When?" I patted my pockets, looking for my car keys. Nothing. I ran toward the stairs before remembering William had driven me to the cabin.

Shit. William. I had to tell him, get him to take me back to town. I pivoted, heading for William's office even as Ford relayed the instructions left by Mafia Hit Man or maybe Balding Blond Guy to meet them at an abandoned garage a few miles outside of Cody.

"Call my brother," I ordered Ford. "Let him know—" What? What could I possibly tell James? That I had the situation under control? Tell him to call the police? If the police were a viable option, wouldn't William have already taken that path? "Shit. Figure something out." I disconnected the call and burst through the office door.

William leaped to his feet at my entrance and took two steps forward. "What is it?"

"They've got Jeremy. You said they'd be safe, but they have him!"

He narrowed his eyes, but other than that, he didn't seem to catch the seriousness of the statement.

I flashed my phone at him. "How could you let this happen? They have Jeremy. They have my nephew." My voice cracked on Jeremy's name.

"How do you know?"

How could he stay so damned calm? "They left a note. Damn it, William, I have to get back to Cody."

"What did the note say?"

I growled, but it quickly turned to a whine. "We don't have time for this. If you won't take me, at least let me borrow your car."

William gripped my shoulders, holding me in place when I would have turned to leave. "You're not going anywhere. It's a trap."

"I don't care if it's a trap. They have my nephew. He's only six, William. Only six. I can't let anything happen to him."

"I've got people watching your family. Let me make a call—"

I couldn't take any more. "You want to sit on your ass and make a bunch of phone calls? Go for it. Seems to be all you're good for now. In the meantime my nephew is in danger, and I'm not going to stand here and wait for your spy friends to get back to you." I broke free of William's hold and made a dash for the front. William might have been bigger than me, but I was fast. As I sped through the hall, I pulled my shirt off over my head and unsnapped my jeans. By the time I'd reached the door and flung it open, all I had to do was slip my pants off. I wrapped the jeans in the shirt, tying the long sleeves around the bundle; then I shifted.

"Donnie!" I'd barely shaken off the last tingle of the shift before William charged through the door behind me.

If William chased in his car, he'd be able to keep pace with me, but he'd have to grab the keys, start the car, and all that jazz before he could follow. He'd be better off shifting and tracking me that way. A snorting, grunting kind of sound carried through the crisp fall air. So yeah, William the bison was going to come after me. I didn't know how fast a buffalo could run, but I could reach nearly forty-five miles per hour if I put enough effort into it. Buffalo were big, but I suspected they were faster than they looked. I couldn't let William catch me, so I had to be smart. I had to forcefully suppress the fear for Jeremy's safety. I couldn't be smart if I allowed my emotions to overwhelm me.

Bison bulls were big and could reach nearly 1,200 pounds, which meant my advantage was going to be my smaller size. I could get places William couldn't. I changed my trajectory, avoiding the dirt road we'd taken to get to the cabin. Instead I picked a route that led through and wove around thick bushes and trees. The small paths I took allowed me to quickly head in the right direction while keeping William from getting too close.

It wasn't the first time I tried to run through the woods with a bundle of clothes between my teeth, but whenever that had happened in the past, it didn't matter so much if the fabric caught on branches or twigs. The first time a hem caught on a bush, I jerked free without much difficulty. When it happened again, maybe a quarter mile later, the tied sleeves holding the bundle together came apart, spilling my clothes, and more importantly my cell phone, onto the ground.

Never before had I wished for opposable thumbs while in my coyote form. If I wanted to keep my clothes—and that all-important cell phone—I was going to have to reassemble the bundle. I skidded to a stop and darted back to my jeans. I shifted, hissing when the October mountain air assaulted my bare skin. I grabbed the jeans and patted at the pockets. Shit. No phone.

William huffed and puffed in the distance, more like the fairy-tale big bad wolf than a buffalo. He was close—closer than he should have been. Clearly the bushes and brambles weren't slowing him down much. Maybe he was faster than the average buffalo?

I dug through dead leaves and pine needles on the forest floor, searching for my phone. How hard could it be to find a piece of shining silver in the middle of muted browns and greens?

The *clomp, clomp, clomp* of William's hooves grew closer. I couldn't see him yet, but there was no doubt he was nearer than was good for me.

I swept aside another pile of dead vegetation, my fingers sliding against cool metal. Finally! I grabbed my phone and stuffed it into the pocket of my jeans. Then I rolled the jeans into a bread-sized loaf and wrapped my shirt around it again. I tied off the sleeves and shifted to my coyote form just as William squeezed between two fir trees not ten yards from me.

I knew the timing kind of sucked, but he was impressive. I hadn't spent much time around buffalo, but I was pretty sure William was a prime specimen. Those shoulders, which were awe-inspiring in human form, were King Kong-huge in this form. His massive head, shaggy mane, and hump on his back made him seem as large as a Winnebago bus. Thick horns curled on his head like a crown. He was powerful, majestic.

And pissed. He snorted, and even from this distance I could see the rage in his coffee-colored eyes. He jutted his snout in my direction, nostrils flaring. I'd almost forgotten. Buffalo had poor eyesight, but they had really excellent noses. Even if I was faster than him—something I wasn't really convinced of—he'd be able to track me as easily as I tracked him. Which was why the phone was a critical piece of the plan.

And sitting here staring at him wasn't getting me any closer to Jeremy.

I lucked out a couple of miles later when I found an irrigation ditch complete with culvert. I could use the water to disguise my scent, at least for a little bit. Maybe even long enough to put adequate distance between William and me.

The icy water made me whine as I splashed through. It wasn't particularly deep, and the coyote in me could handle the cold better than human-me could, but the chill pierced deeper than I would have liked. And I was going to need to do more than run through the shallow stream. I dropped my clothes, shifted back to human form, and rolled the parcel in the mud to mask its scent since I couldn't afford for my phone to get wet. Crouching there naked, I tried to catch my breath. The coyote in me could run for miles without stopping, but this shifting back and forth business was taking too much out of me. If I kept it up, I'd be exhausted and useless. Damn that stupid buffalo for making this necessary.

I shifted back to coyote, rolled into the irrigation ditch, making sure to soak my coat, grabbed the clothes again, and ran. Again.

I picked up my pace and took a zigzag path heading roughly east. Soon I'd reach a road or a highway that would take me back to Cody. Back to Jeremy.

"Donnie! Get back here."

I nearly stumbled to a halt at the distant shout. William must have shifted back to human, which meant he'd given up the chase. Did he think he could simply order me back to him?

"It's not safe!"

Again, I nearly stumbled to a stop. That wasn't what I expected to hear. Was he really worried about my safety?

I squeezed off those thoughts. I had to keep going.
I didn't have a choice. I couldn't face James or Janey
again if I let something happen to Jeremy. It didn't matter
if it was dangerous to me. And if William had been so
concerned with my welfare, he should have just driven
me like I asked. No way could I sit around in safety while
my nephew was facing who knows what.

I dug my paws in, trying for another burst of speed.

Fifteen minutes later I shifted again. It took way
longer than it normally did—long enough I was afraid
I wouldn't be able to shift at all. I flopped onto a bare
tree stump, every joint and nerve in my body aching.
I fumbled my way into the crusty, muddy mess that
was my clothes and pulled out my phone. I found the
number I needed.

"Ford? Can you pick me up? And bring me some
clothes?"

IT took Ford forty minutes to get to me.

I'd considered walking down the highway a ways,
maybe skim a few miles off the distance Ford had to
drive, but I was so tired from the multiple shifts, I could
barely move. Hunger gnawed at my gut to the point of
nausea, and I'd have sold my left nut for a sip of water.
I'd have given *anything* to sleep. Instead, I pulled on
my mud-crusted clothes and waited.

The gamble for me had been on who would show
up first. Ford or William. William wasn't stupid. He
might have lost me in the woods, but he knew I'd have
to go back to Cody, and there weren't a lot of choices
on how one could get there. He might have assumed I'd
run there the whole way in coyote form, but I doubted

it. He was a shifter too, and he knew how many shifts I'd done and what the impact would be.

The rumble of a battered half-ton pickup brought me struggling to my feet, relief rushing through me. Ford. Finally.

The passenger-side window rolled down. "You look like shit."

I looked at him balefully. "Duh." I opened the truck's door and examined the distance between the floorboard and the ground. This was going to suck.

Concern flashed across Ford's angular features, but he didn't offer to help. Smart man. With the ease of an arthritic octogenarian, I climbed into the seat.

"Your clothes." Ford pointed at a plastic grocery sack on the floor by my feet before putting the truck into gear.

I leaned back, reluctant to make any move now that I was settled into the relative comfort of Ford's passenger seat.

Ford pulled a folded piece of paper from his pocket. "Here's the note."

My mouth went desert dry as my hand clenched almost compulsively around the paper. It was a typical eight-and-a-half-by-eleven-inch sheet, folded in half. I lifted the top flap, and my heart seized. Someone, probably Balding Blond Guy, had copied a picture of Jeremy near the monkey bars at his school's playground. Mafia Hit Man held Jeremy against him with one hand, his other hand resting on the butt of a lethal-looking black handgun. Jeremy's eyes were wide with fear, and he leaned as far away from Mafia Hit Man as he could, given the man's grip.

How could William—*how could I*—have let this happen? Above the picture, in bold, all caps Times New

Roman, was my name and an address, then the words
"COME ALONE." They might as well have added "Or
else…." The threat was clear.

I recognized the address on the note. The abandoned
garage was the only building still standing on that city
block.

Better to keep people from hearing the screams?

"Did you call James?" I tried to redirect the conversation.
Staying focused on the mission, so to speak, was the only
way I'd be able keep from freaking out completely.

"Tried. No answer."

"Janey?"

Mouth pinched, Ford refused to look at me. "Same.
No answer. And before you ask," he said, before I could
ask, "I also tried your father and your other brothers.
No one is answering their phones."

"Do you think they were kidnapped too?"

Ford shrugged. "I don't know. I mean, if they'd
taken the rest of your family, why would they only tell
you about Jeremy? On the other hand, it seems too
coincidental that no one is answering their phones."

I scrubbed at my face, knocking a dried leaf out of
my hair. "Damn it."

"You need to call the cops."

"I can't." I pulled the bag up and tried to figure
out how I was going to change clothes in the cab of a
pickup. "These guys aren't messing around. I can't let
them hurt Jeremy." I tightened my grip on the bag so
hard my fingertips tore through the plastic.

Prickles built behind my eyes. I shut them in
automatic defense. Getting all teary wasn't going to do
Jeremy any good.

"If the police can't handle these guys, what do you
think you can do?" Ford took his eyes off the road for

a minute. "No offense, man, but you're in no shape to be taking on some guys who resort to kidnapping. I'm not even sure you're in any shape to do anything except take a nap."

I scrubbed at my face. "I don't know what I'm going to do. I just know I can't do nothing."

He pursed his lips but didn't try and talk me out of my nonplan. He probably knew it wouldn't do any good. He knew me better than anyone else. He cursed under his breath. "There's a couple of protein bars in the glove box. Eat them. They won't be much help, but it's better than nothing."

My mouth started watering at the thought of protein bars, so I wasted no time in opening the glove box and pulling them out. My fingers trembled while I tore open the first bar's packaging. I barely stopped to chew. It honestly felt like the nutrients in the surprisingly tasty bar absorbed straight into my system. The foggy feeling in my head lessened and a little energy seeped into me.

I decided to let the first protein snack digest a bit before noshing on the other. I pulled off my crusty shirt and swapped it out for the one Ford brought with him. Ford's lips curled a bit when flakes of mud and dried leaves fell onto his floor mat, but he didn't say anything. He tended to err on the side of neat freak more often than not, but he must have chosen to overlook the mess for the moment. I pulled the shirt over my head, then eyeballed the jeans. Ford's truck wasn't really big enough to make changing pants anything less than awkward.

"So no plan." Ford kept his head facing forward while I unbuckled the seat belt and squirmed out of my jeans.

"Not a plan, no. I'd call it more of a quasi-agenda. Like bullet points. Or, well, a bullet point." I kicked the dirty denim off my feet, then bent forward to shove my legs into the clean jeans.

"No." Ford's voice was absolute.

"No?" I grunted, arching my hips to hitch the jeans over my bare ass.

"No. You are not trading yourself for your nephew."

I sagged into the seat, the simple act of getting dressed having exhausted me. "That's not my bullet point."

I'd had no idea Ford could do side-eye so well. I cleared my throat. "It's not all of the bullet point. While I'm doing that, I need you to make a few calls."

His lip curled.

I tore into the second protein bar. "You're my best friend, and I need your help. *Jeremy* needs your help."

He cursed under his breath. "Low blow, Donnie."

"I can't afford to play nice." Not like he wouldn't have helped me without the guilt trip. He growled a lot, but it was for show. Usually.

He shook his head, disgust twisting his expression. "Why don't you make the phone calls and we let the police make the meet with the bad guys? Shit, listen to me. That's how messed up this is. I actually used the phrase *bad guys*, like it was a regular thing."

"I don't know who I can trust. For all I know, these guys can track our phones." I hadn't thought of it before, but now I thought it might be a real possibility. "Crap. Go to Walmart and pick up one of those TracFone things, the ones you don't need a plan for. I need you to call Jesse."

"Your ex?"

"Yeah. He may have connections with the other hotels in the area. Have him poke around. I need to find out if anyone has seen Mafia Hit Man or Balding Blond Guy. I'm not sure where to focus beyond that, though. I mean, these guys are here on a mission, so they probably want to stay somewhere out of the way, but on the other hand, they don't seem the type to put up with grungier, more rustic choices."

I shoved the last of the protein bar into my mouth.

"And while I'm playing telephone detective with your ex-boyfriend, you're going to do something stupid, like surrender to a couple of thugs who have no compunction about kidnapping little boys and maybe their entire family. What do you think they're going to do to you?"

My stomach rolled, making me regret the protein bar. I didn't want to think about it. "Doesn't matter. If there's even the slightest chance I can save Jeremy from this, I'm going to try."

Ford started to say something, but I held up a hand. "Let it go. You can't change my mind. Take me to the apartment so I can get my car. Then make some calls. And Ford?" I leaned against the headrest, closing my eyes in an attempt to gather as much rest and peace as I could in the short time before I was going to willingly walk into a den of bad guys. "Don't follow me. I need you to be the backup plan."

"Backup plan?"

"If I don't get out, then it might be a good idea to bring the cops in. But until then, I don't want these dudes to get twitchy. Better not to tempt them. Or threaten. Or whatever they'll be if the cops show up." I closed my eyes in exhaustion. I didn't even know what I was saying anymore.

I thought I heard Ford mutter "They'll be arrested," but he'd said it quietly enough I didn't think I was supposed to hear. It was okay. I had bigger things to worry about.

Chapter Twelve

MY damp palms slipped on the steering wheel as I maneuvered my piece-of-shit car onto the crumbling asphalt parking lot. I parked the car and steeled myself with a deep breath. As soon as I opened the door, I knew my single-bullet-point agenda was going to fail in a big way. The whole plan to rescue Jeremy was predicated on the bad guys actually having Jeremy. But he wasn't there.

A number of odors floated on the air. Oil. Grease. Burnt rubber. Urban decay and violence. No trace of coyote pup and peanut butter, which made up the base scent of Jeremy. Either they were keeping him somewhere else—which would make an exchange unlikely—or they didn't really have Jeremy. Neither was an optimistic option.

I stepped back, intending to get into my car and reevaluate my single-bullet-point agenda. The crunch of gravel on asphalt told me it was too late for that plan.

"It took you long enough."

I didn't need to turn to know Mafia Hit Man stood behind me. The tang of gun oil also told me he was armed.

I almost stopped breathing when I caught the iron-rich hint of blood.

I rushed toward Mafia Hit Man, uncaring of the gun pointed at me. "What have you done to my nephew?"

His eyes darted to the left. "Nothing. For now. If you want to keep it that way, you'll have to cooperate."

Now that I was close enough to him, I saw the blood I'd sensed was his own. He looked like he'd gone a round or two with a grizzly. Scratches marred the skin of his neck, and a black eye bloomed on the right side of his face. Under Mafia Hit Man's blood and his own stink, I caught the slightest whiff of Jeremy, but it was faint. Almost too faint for them to have done more than brush up against each other.

"It takes a certain level of lowlife to use a kid." I tried to mask my worry with bravado. "If anything has happened to him…."

The jerk didn't even blink at my implied threat. "Tell us where to find Bryce and no one else needs to get hurt."

"Bryce?" Did I even know anyone named Bryce?

"Don't be cute."

It still took me a minute. They meant William, clearly. Funny, I didn't usually think of him that way. "Let me see my nephew and arrange for him to be taken somewhere safe, and I'll tell you whatever you want."

"This isn't a negotiation, Mr. Granger."

"I'm not negotiating. I'm telling you what needs to happen if you want my cooperation." Which, now that I thought about it, was pretty much the definition of *negotiation.* "I see my nephew, ensure his continued safety, or you guys can go fuck yourselves."

"You should reconsider your demands."

Ice water sloshed in my guts at the cold voice. I'd been so focused on Mafia Hit Man, I hadn't noticed anyone else approaching. The skin on the back of my neck crawled, and I knew I was going to be in big trouble.

I glanced over my shoulder, and a six-pack of creeps stood behind me, each one holding a gun of one kind or another.

Shit. I hadn't expected this level of reinforcements. Which meant my agenda really wasn't the best plan I'd ever concocted.

One man stood slightly in front of the rest, with Balding Blond Guy to his right. He didn't seem any older than William, and he was better-looking than someone who associated with kidnappers should be. Blond hair was combed back in a style that made it look like he'd just walked out of the salon, and a calf-length camel coat waved jauntily in the breeze. Actually, he looked like he belonged on some magazine spread selling watches or high-end trench coats or something. What he absolutely did not look like was someone who would hire a couple of brutes to kidnap six-year-old boys.

Something about his light French accent made me think of snakes slithering through dead bushes. If I had to hazard a guess, I'd say this was Robert Conrad. Or, if not the man himself, someone high enough in the organization that these guards he surrounded himself with deferred to him.

"Bring him inside," Boss Man said, gesturing between me and the garage.

Somehow I didn't think that would be a good idea.

The men took a step forward. I took a step back.

I danced to the right. They followed.

I stopped and waited. They moved.

I didn't know what else to do, so I cut and run. I'd never be able to outrun a bullet, but a moving target had to be harder to hit than a stationary one. I barreled toward Mafia Hit Man. Simple probability stated I'd have a better chance getting past the single dude with a gun than the six-pack with assorted weapons.

Deep inside, I knew I'd already lost the bet. I was screwed the minute I raced out of the cabin by the mountain without a plan. I didn't have time to obsess about my poor decision-making. Mafia Hit Man threw out his arms in an attempt to stop my forward charge, but I ducked and twisted, avoiding his grab. He flailed about for a moment, and I elbowed him in the short ribs as I pushed past, making him drop his gun.

I didn't have time to celebrate my minor victory, though.

I should have been fast enough. On normal days I could run faster in human form than most athletes. But after my chase through the woods and the back-to-back shifting, I was done in. My attempt to dig my toes in and eke out a smidgen more speed only managed to knock me off-balance.

A muted *pop* sounded, and I ducked my head as a projectile of some sort passed by with a small concussion of air. It didn't have the heat or speed of a bullet, but I didn't have the time—or the knowledge for that matter—to analyze the weapon. A second later another muted *pop* sounded, followed almost immediately by a pinching sting in my neck.

Aw damn. My shifter metabolism—a gift when it comes to binging on carbs—managed to push the drug, a sedative of some kind, through my body at top speed. It wouldn't last—my metabolism, again—but it would incapacitate me long enough for these creeps to get their hands on me.

Even as the thought reached me, it faded away like a wispy cloud in the noonday sun. My legs thickened, my stride shortened as the drug took effect. I tripped on air and sprawled on the asphalt, scraping my chin, hands, and knees on the rough surface.

I stared at my scraped hands, cross-eyed. The world twisted around me, and my eyes tried to follow. No matter how hard I tried, I couldn't get my eyes to focus. Finally exhaustion, the drug, or eyestrain dragged me into unconsciousness.

THIS must be what a hangover felt like. I blinked my throbbing eyes open, wincing when the dim light stabbed my corneas. Until this moment I hadn't known my corneas had a direct line to my brainstem. But I'd never had a hangover. Shifters didn't get them. Our bodies processed alcohol faster than a human's did. Also important to note: I hadn't had anything to drink. Had I?

I tried to sit up, but my body didn't cooperate. It took a second to realize duct tape secured me to a metal folding chair. What the hell was going on? Why couldn't I think?

The quiet murmur of male voices broke through the static in my brain. "Any sign of Bryce?" one man asked.

"None. Men are keeping watch, but so far he hasn't shown."

A growl vibrated in my chest at the sound of Mafia Hit Man's East Coast voice. Now I remembered why I was here. Those jerks did something to my nephew, then to me. They'd hit me with some kind of trank dart.

The folding chair beneath me creaked, and I stilled my squirming.

"When can we question that one?" Mafia Hit Man continued, apparently missing the noise.

"Another hour or so. The darts were calibrated for a man of Bryce's size, so it might take Granger a little longer to come to."

Okay. They thought I was still out. That would help. I tilted my head, hopefully slowly enough not to draw attention to myself while being far enough to get a broader view of the room.

I didn't think they'd taken me too far. Probably I'd been tied up in the mechanic's shop of the abandoned garage.

"Think he'll talk?" Mafia Hit Man sure had a lot of questions. I couldn't complain, though—if they talked to each other, they wouldn't pay attention to me. And maybe I'd learn something useful before they killed me.

"I'm sure of it. Jim's bringing Vasquez. If Granger won't talk to me, Vasquez will get the info." I finally recognized the voice of Conrad—or at least the guy who I suspected to be Conrad.

Mafia Hit Man grunted. "That'd do it. I've heard Vasquez could convince a corpse to share its secrets."

I'd fully checked the area to my right and didn't catch sight of anyone.

I flopped my head to the left, moving a little faster than caution might have suggested I should. If they were bringing in some guy who scared Mafia Hit Man, I was pretty sure I didn't want to be there long enough to meet him.

The other side was clear. Light spilled through an office door window, two men silhouetted in the frame.

Maybe getting free would be easier than I thought.

With the duct tape, shifting would be a bitch—fur and adhesive was a bad combination—but it wouldn't be impossible. I'd shift and run to town. I'd find William or call the cops or something. It rankled to admit it, but Ford—and William, if I was being honest—had been right. I wasn't equipped to handle folks like this on my own.

A phone chimed in the office. A couple of seconds later, Conrad said, "Vasquez will be here in ten."

It was officially time to skedaddle.

I closed eyes and tried to shift. And tried again.

Nothing.

This had never happened before. Ever. Shifting from one form to the next had been as easy as walking. I told my legs to move, and they did. I told my body to shift, and it did. But not this time. It was like reaching for a mirage. I could almost see it, but the reality of it escaped my grasp. I concentrated on the image of my coyote. Dusty-brown-colored fur, with a tail a shade closer to gray. Lean body, four long legs.

Nothing.

What happened to me? Why couldn't I shift? Had there been something in the sedative they'd shot me with? My breathing sped up so much I was nearly hyperventilating in panic. My vision faded to silver at the edges. I needed to calm down. To think. If I kept it up, I'd probably pass out from lack of oxygen, and that wouldn't do anyone—least of all me—any good.

Think, Donnie, think.

I caught a scent of something in the air. Something familiar. Something herbaceous. It was like William and sagebrush and pine. It hit me. The reason I couldn't shift was because of my mad dash from the cabin and the multiple changes. I'd literally worn myself out. The protein bars I'd eaten weren't enough to fully recharge my energy; then the sedative these freaks had dosed me with…. There was debate among shifters about whether shifting was magical or physiological. Either way, shifting shape was all about energy, and I was a freaking dead battery.

I must have made a sound, because before I could figure out an alternative escape plan, footsteps echoed through the empty garage. Boss Man, Mafia Hit Man, and Balding Blond Guy marched toward me. I hadn't even known Balding Blond Guy was there with them.

Conrad stopped a couple of feet in front of me. "Good, you're conscious."

Since any pretense at being passed out was likely to be useless, I straightened in the seat. No need to showcase how anxious I was, right? Also, this new position made it easier to see what was happening around me. Apparently it had been a good thing I hadn't shifted and run. The same six-pack of guys who'd accompanied Conrad before still hung around. Only they weren't in the building with us; they stood in pairs in the parking lot. Their presence would have made my escape a little difficult, especially if they'd seen me shift.

"I can't say much about your décor." This time when I looked around, I made it as obvious as I could. Hopefully they'd think I was just being snarky or full of bravado, when really I was trying to catalogue as many details as I could. I had to find another way out. The nanosecond they gave me an opening, I was moving.

Hopefully before Vasquez showed up. I suspected I would not enjoy whatever tools this Vasquez character would employ to get me to talk.

Mafia Hit Man and Balding Blond Guy glared at me, but Boss Man simply arched a brow and asked, "Do you find yourself amusing?"

I shrugged, the duct tape pulling tight around my bound arms. "Sometimes. Usually." I really hoped I didn't sound as scared as I felt. Of course, if I did, I'd probably be rocking in the corner with my thumb in my mouth.

Maybe some of the fear showed through. Conrad tucked his hands into the pockets of a designer suit that had no business in an abandoned garage in Cody, Wyoming. "You can make this a lot easier on yourself if you just tell us where we can find Bryce."

"Where's my nephew?" I countered.

Mafia Hit Man pulled out a gun. "Where's Bryce?"

"I don't know. Believe me, if I knew the answer, don't you think I'd tell you? You have my nephew, and William seems like the type who can take care of himself."

"Earl," Conrad said, nodding at Mafia Hit Man, "seems to think you care for Bryce, and that he cares for you. Yet you want me to believe you don't know where he's hiding."

"Earl," I said with my own nod to the man, "is full of it. It doesn't matter if I care about William. Unless he felt the same way—which he doesn't—he'd have no reason to keep me apprised of his whereabouts."

A flurry of movement erupted just past the corner of my eye. I blinked, and a second later one of the pairs of guards in the parking lot had disappeared.

Mafia Hit Man swung out, fist connecting with my face. Pain exploded in my cheek, and the impact

knocked me, chair and all, back. My head banged on the
cement with a crack that echoed through the room. Or
that might have been the sound of my brain bouncing
against my skull.

"What the hell was that for?" I asked as soon as I
could form the words. I spit blood from my split lip to
the pavement in front of me. Which, since my cheek
practically touched the cement floor, meant the blood-
spit mix pooled about three inches from my nose.

"I don't think you're taking this very seriously, Mr.
Granger." Conrad crouched near my head, bracing his
arms on his bent knees, all casual and shit.

I glared up at him. "I take it very seriously. But,
really, I don't know what you want from me. I don't
have the information you want. William doesn't know
me very well, so he's hardly likely to tell me where his
secret clubhouse is. I don't know where he is." I made
sure my voice trembled a bit. Not that I needed to fake
being nervous. The anxiety was 100 percent present.

"That's too bad." Conrad nodded at Mafia Hit Man
and Balding Blond Guy. The two goons each gripped
an arm and hauled me, chair and all, upright.

I caught another flash of movement, and one of
the other pairs of guards seemed to vanish. I shook
my head. Maybe my skull hitting the concrete had me
seeing things?

"You brought me in for this?"

My nuts drew up protectively at the rich female
voice. Women don't usually give me the willies—just
because I don't want to sleep with them didn't mean I
had any antifemale hang-ups—but the combination of
cold amusement and that velvety contralto terrified me.
Or maybe it was her scent. She was completely human,
I'd have sworn it, but she smelled cold and musty, like a

snake coiled to strike. I hadn't thought there was an odor more off-putting than the urban decay and violence that surrounded Mafia Hit Man and Balding Blond Guy. Boy, had I been wrong.

I stopped breathing and sat absolutely still, an instinctive reaction to prey facing a predator, with nowhere to run.

"Vasquez," Conrad greeted the woman, his tone awfully deferential.

It shouldn't have surprised me. At all. But finding out that the person Conrad brought in to torture information out of me was a woman had me jerking my head up to meet her eyes. Big mistake.

She was an unassuming woman, a little on the plain side, with round features, dark hair, and big eyes. Eyes that assessed me like a frog on a biology table. Eyes as dead as that frog's.

"You brought me in for a kid? You're losing your touch, *Bobby*." She stressed his name in a way that made me think it was an insult.

Conrad ground his molars together; I could see the twitch and strain in his jaw. Finally he squeezed through gritted teeth, "Robert." He said his name the French way, eliminating the final *t* sound and drawing out the last syllable like "air."

For their part, Mafia Hit Man and Balding Blond Guy were as intimidated as I was. They shuffled back a couple of steps, letting Conrad face her on his own.

"He's been surprisingly tight-lipped."

She rolled her eyes, her expression clearly saying *amateurs* even if the only words she spoke were "I'll need my case."

When no one moved, she snapped her fingers, and Balding Blond Guy hopped to it, dashing out the side door.

"I don't know anything," I blurted out.

"We'll find out." Vasquez smiled, and I changed my opinion about her dead eyes. They weren't dead now. They practically glowed with evil anticipation.

As we waited for Balding Blond Guy to return, cold seeped into my body, fingers first. Soon it felt like I was standing outside in the middle of January. That must be what panic felt like. But I'd been scared before, and this chilled, chattering thing hadn't happened. The tips of my fingers tingled, and goose bumps prickled over my arms.

"What's taking him so long?" Vasquez demanded, glaring at the doorway through which Balding Blond Guy had exited.

"I'll find out—" Balding Blond Guy came sailing though one of the half-open garage bay doors, cutting off Mafia Hit Man's offer. Balding Blond Guy skidded across the pitted concrete and came to a halt at Conrad's feet.

We all stared down at him for a second. He was breathing, but that was about all I could tell. Almost in sync, Conrad, Vasquez, Mafia Hit Man, and I looked to the garage door. The broad form of a man stood highlighted by the ruby glow of sunset. I'd recognize that shoulder-to-waist ratio anywhere. I'd spent the last several months memorizing every angle and curve.

William.

My first reaction was relief. William was here. I would be safe.

My second reaction was hope. William was here. He could find and rescue Jeremy.

My third reaction was anger. What the hell was he doing here? Weren't we trying to keep the bad guys from finding him?

"It seems gossip was correct." Conrad stepped forward. "I hadn't expected you to be dumb enough to come to me, though."

"No shit."

Mafia Hit Man turned toward me, which meant I'd said that out loud. Obviously William wasn't the only idiot in the garage.

"You weren't stupid enough to come alone?" Conrad made a show of looking around.

I looked around too. Had William come alone? He wouldn't have been that stupid, would he?

"You should have stayed in Europe." I nearly sighed at the familiar, professorial sound of William's voice. To hear him, there was nothing to indicate that he faced off against a handful of armed men and women. At least one woman. Which reminded me. Where had Vasquez gone to? She'd been right there a minute ago.

"I had some business to take care of." Conrad stepped forward. It took me a second, but then I realized what he was doing. Conrad drew William's attention, which allowed Vasquez to move nearly undetected. While they talked, Vasquez slithered from shadow to shadow, making her way toward William. Light glinted off the edge of a silver throwing knife in her left hand.

My throat seized.

"You should have left Donnie out of it." He sounded so calm, so confident, it took a second for the menace edging the words to sink in.

Conrad chuckled coolly. "Where's the fun in that?"

Vasquez moved another foot closer to William.

William stood in the doorway, a freaking blazing target.

Vasquez lifted her left hand to throw.

I finally found my voice. "*William!*"

The next sequence of events happened in a simultaneous jumble.

I tried to lunge forward in an instinctive move to protect William, though I was stymied by the duct tape and metal folding chair.

Mafia Hit Man swung a matte metal gun in my direction.

William drew his own knife from goodness only knew where, spinning toward Vasquez.

Four men in black SWAT gear charged in via the same exit Balding Blond Guy had left through, their assault rifles pointed at Conrad and Vasquez.

Vasquez pivoted, flinging her knife. Not at William, but at me.

The knife landed high on my chest, nearly at the armpit. Icy cold fire stabbed into me even as my head slammed against the concrete for the second time, and my vision started to blur at the edges.

The last thing I saw before I passed out—again— was William charging forward, pushing past Vasquez, every inch the torqued-off buffalo heading my way.

Chapter Thirteen

I REALLY needed to stop passing out. It didn't matter that the first time I'd been drugged and the next stabbed; it was wreaking havoc on my self-esteem.

My shoulder didn't hurt, which I counted as a total bonus. On the other hand, I couldn't feel my arm at all, which was a little worrisome. My eyes didn't want to open either. The combination scent of antiseptic and apprehension told me I was in some kind of medical facility. Which really sucked.

"I can tell you're awake." Warm, rough fingers traced my cheekbone. I turned my head into William's hand, basking in the soft touch. "Why don't you open your eyes?" he asked, this time running his thumb along my eyelashes.

"Don't wanna." I snuggled my face into his hand again.

"Why not?"

"Nervous." My voice thickened with anxiety. I really didn't think I could handle seeing William's expression right now.

"About what?" His voice was so quiet, so comforting, I wanted—no, needed—to see him.

"About how pissed you are."

"Donnie, open your eyes."

I squeezed my lids closed against the temptation.

"Please."

Well, hell. I forced my lashes apart and blinked up into his face. I reached up with my good arm and buried my fingers in his thick beard.

He placed his hand over mine, maintaining the connection. "How're you feeling?"

I took a second to assess. "Well, I'm not real sure. I can't feel my left arm. I have the worst case of cotton mouth I've ever had. But I'm not dead, and clearly you're not either, so there are a couple of positives to balance against the negatives."

"You were lucky. If the blade had been any bigger, you might have damaged something vital. As it was, you missed the major vessels and tendons." He glowered at me. "*Don't* do anything like that again."

I didn't feel lucky. That bitch had thrown a knife at me.

I tried to sit up. William pressed me back, then found the remote that controlled the bed's incline. A few clicks later and I wasn't lying flat anymore. It also let me get a better view of William. He looked a little rough around the edges, but there were no signs of injury.

"What happened after I got hit?" I asked him. Another thought struck. How could I have forgotten? I tried to sit forward again. "*Jeremy.* What's going to happen to my nephew?"

"Your nephew is fine." William pressed me back. Again. "Your whole family is fine. Conrad's men didn't get them."

I let out a ragged breath. "How did they get the picture? What happened at the garage? How did you know where to find me? Who were those men?"

"We'll get to all that. But not here."

I blinked and looked around. He'd brought me to Shifter U's Urgent Care Center, which made sense, I guess. He could hardly take me to a hospital. They wouldn't know what to do with my shifter genes. They'd have been able to patch me up, but the local hospital would have been confounded by the way my body processed any drugs they might have given me. At the college's Urgent Care, at least they knew what to do with my specific biology.

But, though they could handle the medical part of this, William probably didn't want anyone else to find out about his problem with Conrad and his gang.

I nodded my understanding. "Then get me out of here. Because we seriously need to talk."

IT took longer than I'd have wished to get on the road back to the cabin. First I had to see the doctor, who took a last look at the wound below my shoulder. He poked and prodded, and I knew whatever they'd given me to numb the pain was wearing off. It didn't hurt, but it started to tingle. Made me wonder what it would feel like in an hour. Not something I was looking forward to.

The doctor also said I was lucky. The knife hadn't gone in very deep, so it was more of a deep cut than a stab. By some twisted coincidence, the knife wound on my front lined up with the still-healing bullet graze on my back. It had been a tough week for that quadrant of my anatomy. It really was too bad shifters healed nearly human-slow. I could have done with some superhealing mojo about then.

William watched the exam with a stoic expression I'd come to expect from him. But maybe it wasn't quite as neutral as usual. There was a tightness around his mouth and eyes that seemed at odds with the blank face. I hissed when one of the doctor's probes sparked something deep in the stab wound. William flinched, his lips tightening even more.

"Refrain from shifting for at least a week. Longer would be better, but with the full moon next week, I know it's useless to expect more."

Dr. Taylor was an owl shifter, so he understood the draw of the moon.

The nurse came in with shifter-specific wound-care instructions; then William bundled me off to his soccer-mom vehicle.

We'd driven for about ten minutes when I couldn't take the suffocating silence any longer. "How'd you know where I was?"

"Ford called."

"What?" I jerked forward, ignoring the unpleasant pressure of the seat belt against the no-longer-completely-numb injury. "That bastard called you?"

"Careful." William placed his large hand on my knee. "It's not like you gave him much choice."

I grunted and slumped back into the seat. "I guess. I'm a little surprised he called you, though, and not the police."

"He realized the police would be out of their depth, even if they had believed him." He glanced at me from the corner of his eye. "It is a bit unusual. The biggest challenge was keeping him from coming along."

The thought of Ford walking into that garage, possibly getting hurt because of me, gave me chills. "How did you stop him?"

William grimaced. "I tied him up."

My eyes widened. "Seriously? Are you out of your mind? He could have fried you!"

At William's incredulous expression, I explained. "He's a *thunderbird*. Like, he controls thunder and lightning, and he does this weird shit with energy fields. Seriously, he could have fried you."

"I thought thunderbirds were myths."

"And they want you to think that. So, really, you can't tell anyone." I shook my head at William's close call. At some level, Ford must have trusted William to get to me. He'd have zapped William, secret identity be damned, if he hadn't. "I wonder why he didn't just shift out?" No matter how big his bird, shifting should have altered his mass enough to get free.

"If you tie their arms right, bird shifters can't change without doing damage to their wings."

I hadn't known that. "I hope you told him that so he didn't try to get out."

"I did. He's not very happy with me right now."

"I bet." I wiggled, trying to make myself more comfortable.

"Why didn't you shift? I saw enough to know you weren't watched the whole time."

I hesitated. I didn't want to admit to him what an idiot I'd been. Or to tell him he'd been right. He'd be completely unbearable. But I didn't lie well, and I wasn't very good at deflection, so I gave in. "I couldn't. I'd shifted too many times already today, plus the run through the woods." I darted a look to see how he reacted. I'd been running away from him, after all. His jaw twitched, but he didn't say anything. "I couldn't shift to save my life at that point. Literally. Then the trank they gave me…." I shrugged. Which was stupid. The throbbing of my chest muscles redoubled.

The hand on my knee squeezed, and I took comfort in it. He understood and, at least for the moment, he wasn't going to comment on my impetuous behavior.

We passed another couple of minutes in silence. With the pain medications almost completely out of my system and no longer fogging my brain, worry over my family returned in a flood.

"What happened with Jeremy? Why couldn't Ford reach my brother?"

William steered the car off the highway and onto a smaller, unnamed road. "Your family is being watched. When Conrad's men approached Jeremy, some of the guards I had watching over your family intervened. Conrad's guys got the picture, but nothing else. In fact, I don't think they intended kidnapping at all. Why take a picture in the middle of the park when they could have just snatched him?"

Relief flooded through me. Jeremy really was okay. "So why couldn't I reach my family?"

For the first time, William seemed guilty. "I hacked the phone company records and had their lines disconnected due to nonpayment."

He could do that? "But what about their cell phones?"

"Same thing."

Wow. William was a fount of amazing abilities. Sure, some of them skewed a little toward criminal, but that didn't make them less impressive. "So everyone's safe? Everyone's okay?"

He nodded. "Which means your sacrificial move was completely unnecessary, completely dangerous, and completely a waste of everyone's time." And there was the growly William I knew and loved.

"What happened to Conrad and his men? And that Vasquez person? Did the cops get them?"

This time he really did growl. "Incompetent fucks. They got the ones I took care of for them, but Conrad, Vasquez, and a couple of others—including your Mafia Hit Man and Balding Blond Guy—got away."

I slumped in the seat. I'd really hoped this had been the end of it. "This whole thing is your fault, you know."

He scrunched his face. He was probably a little ticked, but I found it adorable. I nipped that train of thought in the bud. Or the butt. Whatever the phrase was. Either way, I didn't have time to focus on that right now. He gripped the steering wheel with white-knuckled hands. "I had it under control. If you hadn't gone off half-cocked—"

"Whoa, dude, stop right there. You could have prevented all of this if you'd just talked with me. If you'd told me—"

It was his turn to interrupt me. "I told you I had it under control. I told you I had people watching your family."

I let out a huff of air. "Fine. There is clearly enough blame to share." I scrubbed my fists over my gritty eyes. "Why is it so hard to share your plan with me? Why do you refuse to let me help? Why, for that matter, do you insist on pushing me away?"

"It's not you—"

Again, I interrupted him. "Don't you dare finish that sentence. Clearly there's something about me you don't trust. Which, okay, I get it. It's not like you know me all that well. But I don't understand why you're going to so much trouble for me. I mean, sure, you're taking care of the situation mostly for you, but you're going way above and beyond on my behalf. You hired people to watch over my family. You're hacking phone companies—can you teach me that, by the way?—and rescuing me from some French dude with a chip on his shoulder and a lady torturer. It can't all be CYA."

"CYA?"

I risked a quick glance to get a read on his expression. Blank. I should have known.

"Cover Your Ass," I explained. "Stop avoiding the question. The only time you don't push me away is when we're messing around, and then you still push me away as soon as the endorphin high has dissipated. I want to know why."

I thought for a minute he wasn't going to answer me. I closed my eyes in frustration or grief, I wasn't sure. I hugged my arms close to my body. He pulled the car over to the side of the road.

"I can't afford you." The soft words were barely audible in the quiet car, but they were powerful enough to stop my emotional retreat.

"That doesn't make any sense."

"You're the only person alive with the power to make me alter my plans."

I settled back into the car seat, pulling my legs up until my heels practically touched my ass. I wrapped my arms around my knees, shielding me from his words. "I don't want to make you alter your plans. I just want to be *part of* your plans."

William shook his head. "I knew someone like you once. Just like you. Vital. Charismatic. Somehow sweetly innocent and sexy at the same time."

Jealousy and anger stabbed me full in the chest. Jealousy for the affection in his voice for someone else. Anger that he judged me based on someone else's actions. Curiosity, though, outweighed both of the other emotions. "What happened?"

William didn't say anything for a minute. Then, his placid professor voice back, he said, "It didn't work out." He put the car into gear and started to pull onto the road.

"Stop," I cried out, emotionally incapable of dealing with this now but unable to help myself. I guess I had some kind of masochistic tendencies since I liked to have my heart ripped out of my chest and torn into itty-bitty pieces.

Stomach sliding like a frog on a frozen pond, I asked, "Is there a future for us? For you and me? I know I can be the king of wishful thinking and all that, but sometimes it feels like maybe there's a chance for us, that maybe you're into me too. Then other times you push me away or treat me like one of your troublemaking, less-than-bright students trying to get an extension on a paper."

When he didn't say anything right away, I rushed on. "I like you. I mean, I *really* like you. I don't know what else to do or say to convince you. But what I need to know is, am I wasting my time? Or your time. Or, I guess, our time. Am I just embarrassing myself? I know I sometimes come off as easily distracted or inconsistent, or whatever, but I swear, I've never felt this way—"

"His name was Jasper."

That stopped my rambling.

"We met in college. To this day I have no idea what he saw in me. He was everything I wasn't—fun, exciting. I've always been a bit boring."

Now there I had to agree with this ex and disagree with William 100 percent. He was the least boring person

I'd met. Sure, he could be a bit stuck in his routines, and yeah, he didn't exactly exude party-animal vibes, but I'd never met anyone more compelling.

"It was flattering. I wasn't used to that kind of attention, and I got attached. Too attached."

Somehow I didn't think his relationship with Jasper ended amicably.

"He was recruited the same time I was. His skill set was different—he could fit in anywhere and people would tell him anything. He was being groomed for a different part of the group than I was—more toward social connection and reading people, less undercover and immersion."

William wasn't in the car with me any longer. Physically he was, of course, but his mind was lost in the past. "We were brought in on a mission in a secondary capacity, since we were still in school and considered trainees. But intel indicated a new trafficking ring was gaining traction with younger people, especially students in high-level technical and scientific colleges. We were sent in to one of the targets to pose as transfer students."

A knot the size of the Rockies formed in my throat at the grief in his voice. I'm not even sure William knew how much pain he broadcast.

"Probability of this university being involved was low, which was why the organization decided it was safe to send in recruits instead of full agents. It was supposed to be a good training opportunity, a chance to see us in the field. Well, probability numbers were wrong; not only was the school a legitimate target, the head of the engineering department was involved. We were supposed to report any information we found to our trainers immediately. Our mission was information gathering only. Not action."

William's hand shook on the steering wheel. I laced my fingers through his and drew our folded hands into my lap, offering what comfort I could. I thought maybe he needed to tell this story, to get it off his chest. When it didn't seem like William was going to keep going, I prompted, "What happened?"

"Our trainers assumed we were just enthusiastic, that we were seeing what we wanted to see. Analysts said low probability, so we must have been overzealous." Bitterness creeped into his voice, and I couldn't say I blamed him. Somehow I was sure William had never been overzealous in his life. Placid, plodding William? Not a chance.

"Jasper was sure we could convince them. All we had to do was get proof. Something they couldn't wave aside."

I closed my eyes. I saw where this was going, and it explained a lot. Jasper had done what William assumed I would have done in the same scenario. I wasn't actually sure he'd have been wrong.

"I should have tried harder to talk him out of it. When I couldn't convince him that we needed to work with the organization—they were the professionals, after all—he started looking for proof. He took risks, got in way too deep. I did my best to keep him safe. I failed."

His face shut down, as emotionless as I'd ever seen it. "Jasper's death became the proof the organization needed."

"What did they do?"

A mirthless smile. "Put a mission together using the information Jasper died to collect. A long game that culminated almost six years later when I took down the weapons-trafficking ring last year."

My heart broke a little. William had spent half the last decade essentially avenging his dead lover. The rest of my emotions were a mixed bag. Anger because William would probably never see past the similarities between Jasper and me to give me a chance. Guilt because of that selfish anger. Grief because of what William had gone through. That was a shit-ton of baggage, and I couldn't expect William to drop it for me. But, man, I really wanted him to.

"So that's why you refuse to let me help find out where Conrad and the delinquent duo are staying."

"You're so much like him," William said. "Rushing into danger to do what you think is right, no matter the consequences to yourself. I tried to keep you out of it, to keep you safe."

"It was my choice."

"Your choice nearly got you killed. Twice!" He looked away for a second, and when he'd turned back to me, he had his blank mask back in place.

I stared at our clasped hands, examining the way his slightly darker skin and bigger fingers contrasted with mine. "I understand. I do. But I can't let you wrap me up and put me on a shelf."

"And I can't watch you get hurt."

The small spark of hope, the one I tried really, really hard to keep buried, dwindled a little more. If we couldn't get past this, we'd never have the relationship I wanted. Knowing he was interested in me, even if a little against his will, made the realization that much more painful.

Stalemate. Again.

Chapter Fourteen

THE stench of burned bread and charred herbs and the sharp chime of the smoke detector greeted us as we reached the cabin. William leaped from his vehicle the moment he'd thrown it into park, and I wasn't far behind him.

The bread. The fucking rosemary-and-thyme bread I'd left in the oven on my mad dash to rescue my nephew. How many hours had it been? I was lucky the whole place hadn't caught on fire. The smoke detector's beeping pierced my brain, thanks to shifter-acute hearing. I clapped my hands over my ears. William winced, but it didn't seem to hit him as hard. He ripped open the smoking oven and turned off the heat. He coughed and tried to wave the smoke out of his eyes.

He pointed from me to the window and from himself to the ceiling. I took this to mean he would deal with the alarm while I let some fresh air in.

We set about our separate tasks until the temperature in the cabin had dropped to match the autumn chill outside and the painful screeching of the alarm had faded to a bad memory. We stood awkwardly facing each other in the cabin's foyer.

"I'm sorry." The words were inadequate. The place smelled like hell, and I didn't think the odor would vanish anytime soon. And even though the smell was the worst of the damage, it didn't change the fact that it could have been much, much worse. And it would have been all my fault. "Tell the owner I'll pay to have the carpets, drapes, and upholstery cleaned to get the smell out. Or whatever. I don't really know what is involved." I wasn't sure what something like that would cost, and I couldn't afford it anyway, but I'd do what I had to.

"It's fine."

I flinched at the brusque words. "Really, I don't want your friend to get mad at you."

He sighed, scrubbing his hands over his face. "It's my cabin, Donnie."

That shut me up. "What?" I looked around the extravagant house. "Why would you lie to me about that?"

He closed his eyes but didn't say anything, and I got it. It was all part of his plan to keep the distance between us.

"I can't. I just can't right now." I turned and trudged up the stairs to the room I'd occupied earlier.

I was tired. Mentally and physically exhausted.

I WOKE three hours later with a nagging headache, a throbbing shoulder, and a new sense of purpose. I couldn't maintain my normal sense of optimism when it came to William. Obviously, things weren't going to work out between us, but it would be too painful to stay locked up with him any longer than necessary. Also true, I'd learned my lesson about running off "half-cocked."

How many times had my father or brothers told me I had to take things seriously? That I had to grow up? Well, today I was taking charge of my future. Maybe not in a way anyone in my family, or even William, would approve of, but it would be done my way.

I trudged down to the living room. It was quiet, had a desk I could settle in at, and best of all, it was on the other side of the house from William. I had an agenda, and getting distracted, especially given William's brand of distraction, wasn't part of it. I dug up a notebook and pen, grabbed my phone, and got to work.

First up: Ford.

"I'm going to eviscerate your boyfriend the next time I see him."

It seemed Ford was still a little ticked at the way William had tied him up yesterday. "He's not my boyfriend."

"Could have fooled me. The way he acted when he found out where you'd gone, I thought you'd finally convinced him."

Don't ask. Don't ask. "Really?" I asked. I seriously had zero self-control when it came to William.

"You know how he's always so quiet?"

I nodded. Not that Ford could see me, but still. "It's infuriating."

"He wasn't quiet. He was frantic. He barely let me get any words in, and I thought he was going to throttle me when he found out I'd actually told you where those guys had your nephew. How is Jeremy, by the way?"

"Fine. I guess. William has guards on him and the whole family. He's even got people watching you."

"I know," Ford growled. "One of them had to come in and get me loose from his little rope trick." He grumbled something else I chose not to understand.

"Forget about that," I said, refusing to let him dwell on it. "I've got a plan."

"Of course you do."

I was actually quite pleased with my plan, a two-pronged approach that would, I hoped, end things once and for all.

"Were you able to get a hold of Jesse?"

"Yeah. He's looking into it. He'll call when he knows something."

"Great. In the meantime, I need you to contact a couple other people. Starting with Buddy."

"Buddy?" Voice incredulous, Ford was practically whining when he continued. "But it's almost winter. You know how he gets."

"Exactly. A grumpy grizzly is precisely what we need."

"You *never* need a grumpy grizzly," Ford muttered, but he sounded resigned. "Fine. Anything else?"

"Yeah. You still have your connection to the aviation club?"

"I'm going to regret helping you, aren't I?"

I snorted. "Not even. Oh, I also need you to go visit James. Call me when you get there."

"Am I calling Buddy and the bird herd first or visiting your brother?"

"Both." I made a quick note on the paper I'd filched from the desk. "Call them on your way to James."

"You're going to owe me for this big-time."

I closed my eyes, wondering if my scheme, one that could easily be considered hare-brained, had a chance in hell of succeeding. "I know."

Twenty minutes later, I made the last note to what I'd dubbed "The Plan." I might not be an international undercover spy guy, but I didn't think the plan was half-bad.

My phone buzzed. Finally! "Hey, James. I need your help."

Chapter Fifteen

PLANS made, I snuck into the kitchen and stopped dead. At some point while I slept and schemed, William had picked up the mess I'd left on his counters. The room still stank of burned bread and herbs, but all the flat surfaces gleamed and chrome appliances sparkled.

Pressure built behind my eyes. I wasn't tearing up, I wasn't. I refused to be affected by his act of kindness. And shame didn't have me swallowing back the heart that had climbed into my throat. Not at all. Not only had I almost burned down his kitchen, but I'd neglected to even clean up after myself. No wonder he thought I was incompetent.

My stomach grumbled, reminding me why I had sought out the kitchen in the first place.

For once I wasn't in the mood to cook. I'd give just about anything for a box of Cap'n Crunch, a pint of milk, and a mixing bowl. Since it was highly unlikely William had a stash of sugary cereal buried in the pantry—he struck me as more of an All-Bran kind of guy—I pulled open the fridge for inspiration.

A pound package of bacon beckoned. Bacon might just be enough of a happy substitute for sugary cereal.

Bacon?

William was a vegetarian. He ate eggs, sure, but bacon? I hadn't questioned the bacon that morning, assuming the cabin's owner wasn't averse to the occasional meat product. But this was William's place.

I closed my eyes and leaned my forehead against the open door of the refrigerator. Me. He had bacon for me.

I didn't know why, but the idea that he'd gone out of his way to buy me bacon, as well as the other meats he'd stashed in the freezer, destroyed the protective shield I'd built around my heart.

Before I had time to second-guess myself, I made my way to the back of the cabin to William's office. He sat exactly where I'd pictured him, but instead of focusing on one computer monitor or another, he leaned back in his chair, eyes closed. It wasn't a peaceful pose; the grooves etched around his eyes and between his brows belied any sign of peace.

"Hey," I said, keeping my voice low. "You should go to bed if you're falling asleep in your chair."

His eyes popped open.

"Unless you're hungry. I could maybe make something. I'll even clean up my own mess," I added.

"I'm fine." He straightened in his seat, wrapping his fingers around the curve of each armrest.

I nodded and edged my way into the room and around to his side of the desk. "Thank you for cleaning the kitchen. I'm sorry I made such a mess."

His fingers twitched like he wanted to reach out, but he contained the motion. "It's fine."

I extended a hand to trace the furrow between his brows. "You look tired. You really should get some sleep."

He shook his head. "I've got work. I'm waiting to hear from—"

I glided my thumb across his lips, silencing him. "Let's play a game."

He quirked an eyebrow at the suggestion. "A game?"

"Yeah. A game of make-believe."

This time his lips quirked in a small smile. "Make-believe."

I nodded, pushing his rolling chair back a few more inches so I could hitch up onto the desk, my dangling legs hanging between his knees. "Let's make believe this whole deal, everything going on out there, doesn't exist. No creepy Mafia Hit Man or crazy assassin chicks out to get you or me. Just you. Just me. Right here. Right now."

"Donnie…." William leaned forward, resting his head on my knee. "I don't know if that's a good idea."

"Probably not," I agreed. "But William?"

He looked up at me.

"I need you. Right now, I need you and I need this."

"Yeah. Me too." William stood, stepping against my body.

I wrapped my good arm around his neck, stretching up until our mouths met.

Our first kiss had happened out of necessity.

Our second happened as a distraction.

This kiss was full of gentleness, of tenderness. And of a quiet desperation that broke my heart a little, even as it filled it with warmth. We might not be compatible for the long haul, but we had tonight and each other. Somehow that would have to be enough.

He led me out of the office, up the stairs, then into his bedroom. If I'd seen the space before now, I'd have known immediately this was William's home. Unlike the town house in Cody or even the rest of the cabin, this chamber was 100 percent William. Two tall bookshelves stood along one wall, with a long chest of drawers between. Framed photographs were arranged in clusters on the walls, and a huge painting of the Grand Tetons hung above the king-size bed's headboard. Almost everything in the room was in shades of brown, from the palest tan to the darkest mahogany. But that picture, with those slashes of orange and pink and blue, indicated a passion, a lust for life the tan walls and coffee-toned duvet couldn't disguise.

We stopped at the foot of the bed with barely an inch separating us. For a minute he simply looked at me and I at him. He cupped my face between his hands and brushed his thumbs along my cheeks, as though memorizing the shape of my face. Maybe, like me, he knew this would be all we could ever have, and he wanted to make a permanent imprint of the moment.

There was no rush when I pulled his shirt over his head, stopping to explore the silky skin beneath, before tossing the fabric aside. It took me a couple of moments longer to discard my own shirt since I had to take more care with my damaged shoulder. When my T-shirt joined his in a heap on the floor, I stepped close and pressed against him, just soaking up the heat and feel of him. He dipped his head, pressing his lips to mine. "Donnie." He sighed my name into my open mouth. Aching and reverent.

I slid to my knees, and he hissed in a breath. "You shouldn't... your shoulder."

"There is no pain in my world right now. Besides, I don't need my shoulder for this." My hands were rock steady as I unhooked his jeans and tugged them to his ankles. I tapped his knee and he stepped free.

I caressed his hard length through his boxers. I didn't want even that thin barrier between us, so I pushed the underwear away. As soon as he was free of that last vestige of clothing, I leaned forward and took him into my mouth. I didn't do anything fancy; I wasn't trying to impress him with porn-star-like skills. I moved my mouth over him with moderate suction and moderate speed, worshipping him with my lips and tongue.

He combed his fingers though my hair, groaning my name. It didn't take long for him to grip a fistful of my hair and urge me to look up at him. I nearly came from the sight of those heavy-lidded eyes blazing at me. "Enough. I won't last."

I thought about repeating his words from the other night—"That's the point"—but since I wanted him in me, over me, I wasn't going to argue.

He helped me to my feet and nudged me toward the bed. He reached into a side drawer and pulled out a bottle of lube.

I lay back against the pillows and beckoned him to me. He braced himself over me, taking his time kissing me, tracing my face, nuzzling my neck. Worshipping me. No one had ever made me feel special like this before. He watched me, my reactions, as if every shiver, every shudder, was important to him.

I was drowning in a cloud of his tenderness and adoration. When his lube-slick fingers pressed between my asscheeks, I sighed and arched into the touch. He sealed his mouth to mine, the fierce, hungry kiss dulling my senses even more. I was floating on instinct, on an inherent drive to be one with William. It wasn't about sex or lust or orgasm. It was about connection and love.

He buried himself in me, slow and deep, and it was everything I could have hoped for. Everything I needed. He reached down and grabbed my legs, then pulled them around his waist. The change in posture pushed him in deeper, and he began rocking.

Our eyes met and held, and I saw in him everything I was feeling. Never before had sex been about anything more than mutual admiration and getting off. But, holy fuck, this was about so much more. He filled a part of me, a part of my soul, I hadn't even known was empty until him. William was going to complete me… or destroy me completely.

He reached down and wrapped his fingers around my cock, pumping in time with his thrusts. The first pulse of my orgasm built at the base of my spine, a slow tingle that grew and intensified with every second. I dug my fingers into William's shoulders and bit my lip, afraid to let out the tsunami of sound that was building along with the orgasm.

William's thrusts got jerkier, faster, and his face reddened with exertion. He came on a groan, his cock pulsing with his release. He still didn't break the eye contact. "Let go," he muttered, dragging his teeth along the column of my throat. "I've got you."

And I fell. Irreparably destroyed. Irrevocably completed.

LIKE the first night I'd spent in his arms, I lay spread across his chest, content as any cat, with William stroking his big hand along my spine. Like a cat, I was ready to purr. I wasn't tired, though in all fairness, I should have been exhausted. But I didn't want to lose this connection, and I was sure, come morning, things would go back to the way they were. So I had to put off morning as long as I could, and the best way to do that was to avoid sleep. Without sleep, morning couldn't come, right?

"Have you thought about going back to school?"

I pushed up from William's chest. Morning might as well have shown up with a bucket of ice water. "What the hell? Why does everyone want me to be something I'm not?" I tried to roll off him, but he'd wrapped his burly arms around my torso, keeping me in place.

He made a soothing sound that caused his chest to vibrate under me. "That's not what I mean. Let me explain, please."

I pressed my lips together, mourning the loss of the shiny, sparkling afterglow thing we'd had going on.

"I came to Buddy's every day because of you."

My breath caught in my throat. "You did?"

He loosened his arms and ran his hands along my hips and sides. "The coffee is good, but nobody's coffee is that good. When I came back to Cody, I was in a dark place. I'd spent years working with some of the worst human beings in the world, pretending to be like them, doing things I wasn't proud of. And suddenly I was Joe Blow professor, normal guy. It was a… difficult… transition. Then one day, I stopped by a hole-in-the-wall café near campus and saw you."

Damn. William needed to seriously stop. Like right now. I was about to bawl like a baby sheep. Or, you know, a lamb.

"You're like that painting." He nodded to the picture of the Tetons at sunrise hanging above our heads. "You're the bright color in an otherwise dull, dark world."

I licked my lips. My voice cracked when I asked, "What does that have to do with school?"

"You're so much better than Buddy's. Let me explain," he hurried to say before I could get offended again. "Buddy's is a great place, and there's nothing wrong with working in a café if that's what you want to do. But, Donnie, the way you bake? The way you cook? Have you considered culinary school? You should have your own shop, run your own kitchen."

The idea thrilled me, I couldn't deny it. But. "It's complicated."

William guided my chin up until I met his dark eyes. I hadn't realized I'd looked away. "How so?"

I propped myself up on his chest so I could maintain eye contact without causing a kink in my neck. "My family is cool with the gay thing. They don't get it, but they don't hold it against me. The fact that I went to college, even for only a couple of years? That they hold against me."

"Because you dropped out?"

I snorted. "Not even. No, they were ticked that I'd wasted so much time and money on college in the first place." I grinned at the way his face twisted up. "Yeah, I'm sure that's practically blasphemy to a college professor like you."

"So they'd think culinary school would be another waste of time and money."

"But wait, there's more," I declared, jabbing my pointer finger into the air with a dramatic flair. "They are also a little offended by my citified tastes."

"Right. Meat-and-potatoes folk."

"You remember." It shouldn't have pleased me he remembered a random comment from the first day I'd finally gotten the courage to approach him with sun-dried tomato and basil scones.

"Everything." The husky timbre of his voice made things deep in my gut coil and squirm in a completely amazing way.

I blinked, trying to stop my hormones from derailing the conversation. "So, yeah, complicated."

William combed fingers through the hair that fell into my eyes. "You've thought of it, of culinary school, haven't you?"

I shrugged. "Sure. It would be cool. But—"

"But?"

"What if they're right? What if it is a waste of time and money? I mean, William, I've never actually stuck with anything before. What if I change my mind after a semester? Or what if I can't cut it? There's a huge difference between baking the occasional scone and actually becoming a pastry chef."

"You're asking yourself the wrong question."

"Then what's the right question?"

"What if you succeed?"

"When people treat you like you're incompetent or wrongheaded your whole life, it makes you wonder if maybe they're right. I've messed up everything else. Why not this too? Besides, I like where I'm at. I enjoy what I do. I've even got Buddy half-convinced to upgrade the bakery and deli choices. Less frozen, more fresh."

William's hands resumed their strokes along my spine. "Don't you want more? When you're capable of so much more?"

Out of nowhere bitterness rose in me. How dare he make me wonder, make me hope? Especially after showing me, time and time again, that he thought me as incompetent as my family did? "No fair. Don't even pretend you think I'm capable of more than what

I'm already doing. Not when you've spent the last two days treating me like an irresponsible child who shouldn't be allowed to cross the street and chew gum at the same time."

"That's not true." William sat up, bringing me with him until I sat straddling his lap instead of being draped over him. "I want—no, I *need*—to protect you. If anything happened to you—"

"It's not your call to make. If you trusted me at all, you'd let me help. Or let me in on the plan, at the very least."

"You know why—"

"Jasper."

He flinched when I said the name, so I gentled my tone. "What happened to Jasper is tragic, but his actions were his, and the consequences were his. I bet he'd be pissed to know you blame yourself. I know I would be. I love you, but—"

It was his turn to cut me off. "You love me?" He looked like I'd just kicked him in the knee even as I gave him a present.

I stuttered out a few inarticulate noises before I could frame words. *Stay on topic, Donnie. Maybe he'll forget you said that.* "That's not the point." I wasn't waiting for him to tell me he loved me too. I wasn't. I knew better. "The point is, I need you to trust me as much as I trust you. If you can't, then I'm not sure what we're doing here."

His fingers shook when he covered my mouth. "You love me?" He watched me like he thought I'd disappear in a second.

I tugged his hand down. "I'm serious, William. I won't let myself be buried in bubble wrap while you fight the bad guys. That's not who I am."

William's eyes were still dazed. I couldn't tell if he'd comprehended anything I said. He kissed my nose. "We'll make it work."

I held my breath. That sounded like a promise.

I felt a faint spark of hope and let William's renewed drugging kisses lull me into the covers.

Chapter Sixteen

A TEXT from Ford woke me up. Or, really, the beeping noise indicating a new text woke me up. I didn't actually know it was from Ford until I'd rolled out of bed—the sadly buffalo-free bed—and dug the phone out of the tangle of my discarded jeans.

Two words. *Found them.*

A second text bubble appeared, this one with an address.

My gut clenched. Jesse had come through. My hands shook, making it hard to punch out my reply.

ME: *Plan B ready just in case?*

FORD: *Yes.*

ME: *Aviation club ready?*

FORD: *Yes.*

ME: *Buddy ready?*

FORD: *Reluctantly.*
ME: *I owe you.*
FORD: *You do.*

I stumbled to the bathroom and splashed water on my face. This was it. Today's the day, and all that happy shit.

The scent of fresh coffee and sagebrush heralded William's appearance in the mirror behind me. He held a red mug in one hand, which he set on the marble counter so he could wrap his arms around me. I closed my eyes and leaned against him, ignoring the guilt eating at me. He was going to be pissed. He was going to disagree with my plan and try to stop me, but I couldn't back away from this.

I focused on the mirror in front of us, of me wrapped in his arms, and etched the image into my brain, so when—if—things fell apart, I'd have this memory to comfort me. If this fell apart, William was going to skin me and turn me into a cap. I soaked up his warmth for a couple of moments longer.

I met his gaze in the mirror, too anxious to meet his eyes without the false distance. "You have contacts with law enforcement, right? People who have the credentials or evidence or whatever they need to arrest Conrad and his men?"

He stiffened. "Why?"

"I know where Conrad and his men are staying."

He didn't pull his hands away, but I felt the distance building between us. "What did you do, Donnie?"

"I had my friend Jesse—the one who works at the Marriott—do some digging. I told you he'd be able to do it."

"I told you to stay out of it." This time his arms did fall away from me as he took a step back.

I didn't drop my eyes from his reflection. "You knew I wouldn't."

His mouth, that amazingly firm, wide mouth that had turned me inside out last night, pursed in clear anger. "Where?" The word cut between us, sharper than any chef's knife I'd ever used.

"Yellowstone Pavilion. A private lodge a few miles out of town. One that caters to high-end tourists who want to play cowboy for a couple of days without getting dirty." I gave him the name and address.

Without another word or look, he turned out of the bathroom, leaving me facing my own bleak reflection. I had no reason to feel guilty. I didn't. This was the best thing for all of us. The sooner we found Conrad's merry band of criminals, the sooner life would go back to normal. What if next time they were able to actually kidnap or hurt Jeremy or one of my other nephews? What if they decided they could kill William from a distance with a long-range rifle or something instead of meeting him face-to-face?

No. It really was better to resolve this whole situation once and all.

As I jumped in the shower, I prayed this didn't blow up in my face like my last plan did.

I MADE french toast. And bacon. The first to comfort, the second to torture. I set a stack of the toast aside for William. I'd made way more than I could eat. Mostly because once I got the griddle going, I couldn't seem to stop until I'd gone through the whole loaf of bread.

I took one bite of bacon before my throat closed. Knowing the package had only been there because William had thought of me, had thought I might like having it, made it impossible to finish a single slice. Damn him. If he'd turned me off bacon, I'd have to hit him. I only hoped I'd have the chance.

I tried to ignore the rumble of William's voice in the other room. It was far enough away I couldn't distinguish actual words, but the tone kept me on edge. He was frustrated. He didn't yell, but every now and then, his tone sharpened.

My phone rang, and I was almost relieved to have something else to focus on. I didn't recognize the number, though.

"Hello?"

"Donnie? There's trouble, man."

At first I couldn't place the panicked voice. Then recognition smacked me upside the head. "*Jesse?*"

This was bad. Very, very bad. Nothing good could have prompted Jesse to call me.

"Yeah. I got a call from my pal Steve. He's the concierge at the Yellowstone Pavilion."

"And?"

"There was some kind of shoot-out. Steve was freaking out, so I don't know the details, but definitely guns fired, sirens blaring."

I slid to the ground, all the strength gone from my legs. "Was anyone hurt?"

"Don't know. Dude, what are you involved in? Ford didn't say anything about people getting shot at."

I scrubbed at my face. It didn't help. "Jesse, you and Steve need to lie low for a while. Seriously. Stay home, or head out of town, something."

"You're really freaking me out."

"I'm freaking myself out too." I sighed and disconnected the call.

Strangely, a sort of calm settled over me. I'd prepared for this. I'd hoped it wouldn't be necessary, but I was ready.

I dialed Ford. "It's time to deploy the troops."

"Fuck."

I couldn't have said it better myself.

My next call wasn't nearly as succinct.

When I'd called my brother the day before, it had been to urge him to take Janey and the boys somewhere safe. I trusted William, and I knew he had people watching, but I wanted them completely out of the way. I'd explained the threat involving Jeremy, terrified the whole time that James would blame me. He didn't. The anger toward Conrad and his men I expected. His demand to be part of the takedown came as a shock. When I couldn't talk him out of it, we brainstormed together. It had been nice not being at odds about things with him. A little weird. I mean, we were talking about bad guys who'd attempted—or at least threatened—to harm his youngest son, and it was sort of my fault. But there was none of his usual I-know-what's-best attitude from him. He'd treated me almost as an equal.

"Did you get Janey and the boys away?"

"I sent them off to her folks for the weekend. They can't get into trouble in Casper. It's too much in the middle of nowhere."

"Good." I bit at my thumbnail, a nervous habit I'd overcome years ago. At least I'd thought so. "Are you sure you want to do this?"

James growled, a sound that was almost scarier in his human form than when he was a coyote. "They threatened my son, my family, you. I want in on their downfall."

His words might have been a little melodramatic, but since I felt the same way, I couldn't blame him. "All righty, then. You got the clothes from Ford?"

One of the major components to Plan B was the resemblance between me and my brothers. Another component was the indisputable fact that we didn't dress anything alike. Both these things were going to let James lure the bad guys out of the city and nearer the cabin. He was going to pick up my car from Ford's and my apartment, wearing my clothes, and head toward the cabin. Hopefully whoever was watching the apartment would follow him. The whole plan kind of hinged on it, in fact.

Once I'd verified my brother understood the plan, I girded my loins and psyched myself up for the next obstacle: William.

I'd barely made it halfway down the hall when it became abundantly clear that William had gotten wind of the situation at the Yellowstone Pavilion. I came to a jerky stop at the eruption of sound from William's office. A furious bellow, followed by the crash of what I could only assume was one of his monitors crashing to the floor. Another crash, this one including the sound of shattering glass, reached me. Crap. This was so not good.

I ran the rest of the way.

William paced the room like, well, like an enraged buffalo. I'd seen William seemingly calm and unconcerned. I'd seen him coldly calculating. I'd seen him frustrated and blustery. I'd never seen him this uncontrolled. I watched from the threshold as he flung his desk chair against a wall, denting the drywall. He flung out his fist, sending the contents of his desk to the floor. For a second, when he swung around and faced me,

I was afraid. In all our previous interactions, he'd never frightened me. Now my mouth dried and adrenaline spiked.

"Blundering, incompetent bastards." He punched his fist into a picture hanging on the wall. The glass from the frame shattered, bloodying his knuckles.

My heartbeat settled a fraction when I realized he wasn't actually mad at me. It was a cold comfort, though. I needed him to be his calm, in-control self for the plan to work. And, honestly, the blood on his hands wrenched my heart; I wasn't equipped to see him hurt, even from some macho thing he did to himself.

I must have made a sound—a nervous squeak, probably—because William stopped his undisciplined trashing of the small room to look at me. He squeezed his hands into fists at his side and closed his eyes, forcing in slow, even breaths.

When his eyes opened again, there was a veneer, however slim, of control. He watched me so closely I thought maybe he was deliberately trying to avoid looking at the mess he'd made. I almost said something about toddler temper tantrums, but sanity won out, mostly due to the understanding that my talent to say the absolute worst thing at the worst time wasn't going to do me a whit of good while at the same time sending him into a wild rampage.

Funny, this moment more than ever illustrated how similar he really was to his alter-animal. Tourists visiting Yellowstone assumed the bison wandering around were as placid and peaceful as a dairy cow. Then something happened, someone got too close to a calf or thought putting a child on a buffalo's back would be the perfect photo op, and the animal proved it could be as wild and protective as a grizzly bear.

"You heard?" I asked, refusing to step away from William, no matter how fiery his gaze or snarly his mouth.

"The teams sent in to apprehend Conrad and his men went in, sirens blaring and lights flashing, as though they'd never done a job before. Men like Conrad don't need much warning to evacuate. He'll end up lost in the wind, and we may never see him again."

I grabbed his forearm. The muscles under my hands were rock solid. He was barely holding himself in check. "I think I know where he's going to be."

He lowered his head and watched me from under his dark brows. Yeah, the pissed-buffalo look worked in his human form too. "How?" he managed to growl from behind clenched teeth.

"We're setting him up."

His eyes flashed, and the disturbing tension in his arms was, well, disturbing me. I released my hold.

"Explain."

I laid out the details of my plan quickly, because the brown of his irises was darkening and bleeding out. He was on the verge of shifting.

"And I thought local law enforcement fucked things up. This is the most hare-brained scheme I've ever heard."

I flinched. I couldn't help it. "I need you to trust me."

"It's not about trust. Donnie, this isn't some kind of movie. The real world doesn't work that way. That many civilians have no business being involved in this. *You* have no business being involved in this."

"You don't want me involved? Too bad. It's too late. I was involved the minute people caught me mooning after your arrogant ass. My fault, not yours, I get it. Believe me, my mooning days are over. But it doesn't matter.

Everything is already moving, and there's no way to stop it. Help us or don't—those are your only options."

I spun around, the cleansing flames of anger fueling my movement.

When this was over, we—William and I—were over. And, you know what? My family could take their doubts and pressure and lack of faith in me and shove it. I didn't need to put up with that crap anymore. They could take me as I am or not, but I didn't need to stay there waiting to be kicked.

But first I'd have to survive the next hour.

Chapter Seventeen

THE plan was really pretty simple.

Step 1—Lure Conrad, Mafia Hit Man, Balding Blond Guy, et al. to the clearing. That was James's job.

Step 2—Herd Conrad, Mafia Hit Man, Balding Blond Guy, et al. into a neat bundle to await the proper law enforcement pickup. That was going to be up to Buddy, me, and the members of Ford's aviation club. And no, the club didn't have anything to do with airplanes or helicopters. They were Shifter U's equivalent of a wolf pack, but for bird shifters.

Step 3—Human law enforcement would pick up Conrad, Mafia Hit Man, Balding Blond Guy, et al.

See? Simple.

I was the first to admit there were a lot of places where the plan could fall apart. For example, weapons traffickers probably had access to weapons. I could only hope that since most of the plan involved shifters in shifted form, they wouldn't think to launch a missile or anything at us. Guns were a worry, but it helped that most of the shifters involved shifted into birds. Birds are a lot harder to shoot than most people expect. Especially people from urban areas who didn't go out duck hunting on a regular basis. Clay and skeet targets followed a predictable trajectory; birds did not. And Buddy, in his grumpy grizzly form, was scary as hell. Most people who ran into a grizzly were too busy peeing their pants to actually do any harm.

Even to me, this sounded very naïve.

I had to comfort myself that everyone involved understood the risks. But they'd all agreed because I asked. That kind of loyalty was a little scary; if anything went wrong, I would never forgive myself.

William met me at his car, and I almost had a heart attack. Instead of mild-mannered professor, he looked like badass secret agent. Black military-style pants with multiple pockets and loops were paired with a long-sleeved black T-shirt that showed off every muscle. The part that had had me freaking out, though, were the guns strapped to his body. Some kind of assault rifle hung across his back by a nylon strap. A matte black handgun of some kind nestled in a holster at his hip. A bigass knife was holstered at his other hip. Damn. My manly man was armed and dangerous.

Clearly he was taking my plan seriously, even if he didn't support it.

My own clothes were much less impressive. I wore black jeans and a dark gray hooded sweatshirt. Maybe I was a little underdressed?

We drove along a small access road until we were about two miles from the clearing. William cut the engine but didn't move to undo his seat belt. He was mannequin-still, but the energy and emotions that emanated from him had a movement of their own. Like him, I kept my gaze fixed in the distance ahead of the SUV. Pressure built, sucking the oxygen out of the car. I was jittery with nerves, and I could barely catch my breath.

"You will be careful."

I jerked at the rough command. The silence had become so all-consuming that the sound of his voice came as a complete shock. I nodded, unlatching my seat belt.

We picked a spot in the brush that had line of sight with the clearing. Then we waited. And waited. The weight of the Rockies settled into my gut, growing heavier the longer we sat there. Even if James had been delayed a couple of minutes, they should have been there by now.

My hand twitched to my pocket, but I'd left my phone in William's car. If a ringing phone disrupted a movie, I could only imagine the chaos of a phone ringing during an op.

How much longer should we wait?

What if Conrad and his crew managed to grab James?

Damn it. I should have made some kind of plan for group communication. Of course, since most of my group was in animal form, nothing short of a banner in the air would be effective.

The temperature dropped a few degrees. And still we waited.

What if the law enforcement people got there before Conrad, Mafia Hit Man, and Balding Blond Guy?

It's not like I always needed to be right. But for fuck's sake, I needed to be right about this.

Thunder boomed in the distance. Damn it, that was all we needed, some fall storm to add *wet* to the *cold and miserable* aspect of this waste of time.

William glanced up into the cloudless blue sky.

The cloudless blue sky.

To the west an eagle whistled. Closer still, an owl hooted.

And again thunder boomed.

"They're coming," I whispered, carefully adjusting my crouched position. Now that it was finally coming down to it, I didn't want any of my limbs to fall asleep on me.

William did that eyebrow thing that meant *question.*

"The thunder." I smiled briefly. "Trust Ford to find a way to get us a message."

He opened his mouth, probably to ask a question more specific than the eyebrow thing, but then there was no time for questions. My beat-up jalopy of a car came barreling into the clearing, sending up plumes of dirt and gravel that were going to play hell on my paint job. Not that I had time to worry about such things. The car fishtailed to a halt and James leaped out, wearing a pair of my jeans and a Cody College sweatshirt. He ran to the back of the car and popped the trunk.

"You ready?" He didn't need to see us to know we were there. Coyote sense of smell and all that. James pulled out my dad's old shotgun and my grandpa's hunting rifle. Since most of our hunting happened on four legs, I wasn't sure why my family had any guns at all, even a pair that were probably antiques. James jogged closer to me, then tossed the rifle in my direction. I caught it awkwardly, staring at the faux wooden stock and shiny barrel. A box of ammo landed at my feet.

William glanced at my tentative hold on the gun. "Do you know how to use that?"

"In theory. I flunked out of hunter's safety when I was thirteen."

"Too busy flirting with Patrick Miller," James said, settling in a couple of feet from me.

I shrugged. "I'm a coyote. Using a gun seemed a little unfair."

William swiped the gun away from me. He reached for the box of bullets, then loaded the gun with a skill I might have admired if bad guys weren't on their way. "In an emergency only," he cautioned, handing the loaded weapon to me.

A pair of golden eagles swooped low, whistling urgently. A pack of wolves howled a couple of miles to the east.

Wolves hadn't been part of the plan.

Neither were the dozen coyotes who burst through the brush on the other side of the clearing, taking up places every hundred meters or so.

Holy crap. Dad? Uncle Mike? Jesus, even my brothers Tim and Andy were there. That was so not part of the plan. Every male in my family—those who were over the age of eighteen, at any rate—circled the clearing.

Before that startling fact had time to process, three black SUVs slid into the clearing, expelling men in black gear surprisingly similar to William's. And they each had an arsenal strapped to their bodies. Three black-clad bodies dashed to my car, guns at the ready. When they found the vehicle empty, they made some kind of hand gesture that I'm sure meant something to someone.

Another man, also in black but in a fancy suit that didn't belong in a Wyoming woods, stepped out of one of the SUVs. Conrad. He didn't appear to be armed. His gaze swept the surrounding area. "There's nowhere to go, Mr. Granger."

I found this to be a bit narrow-minded. Maybe to a city slicker like Conrad there were few options for fleeing, but everyone else there—both four- and two-footed or winged—could make a decent getaway. On the other hand, there seemed to be easily a dozen armed men surveying the area. That could make things tough.

Of course, I didn't say anything. Neither did James, as the comment might have been geared toward him.

"Spread out."

At Conrad's command, ten of the armed men, well, spread out. Mafia Hit Man and Balding Blond Guy stayed close. It was hard to tell it was them by sight, given they were all decked out in SWAT apparel, but I'd recognize their urban-decay-and-violence scent anywhere. The one odor I didn't pick up on was Vasquez. Part of me was glad. Another part of me worried about what that meant.

There was a slightly familiar scent in the mix that bothered me. Human, but lacking that blanket hint of gunpowder and metal the other humans in the clearing carried with them.

One of the bad guys approached the bushes William, James, and I crouched behind. Before he got close enough to pick up on the rust-orange hue of the Shifter U sweatshirt James wore, my brother Tim slinked forward, growling low in his throat and making sure to rustle the dry branches and waist-high grasses. The dude stilled, pointing a lethal-looking assault rifle into the shadows.

I held my breath when the barrel of that gun seemed to pause pointing directly at my brother. Uncle Mike, the coyote closest to Tim and us, howled. The man took a couple of stumbling steps backward and swung his assault rifle in that direction.

"Hey, boss?" one of the men across the clearing said, sounding as worried as the guy near us looked. "I think there's something out there." He nodded to the shadowed trees.

"It's probably a squirrel. What's gotten into you?" Conrad paced a loop around the vehicles, eyes alert. He muttered something under his breath that his subordinate probably wasn't supposed to hear. But thanks to keen shifter hearing, I understood. "Dumb cowards, jumping at shadows."

The guy across the clearing stepped near the trees again. A roar, like tearing leather but louder and more terrifying, ripped through the air.

Holy shit. Where did Ford or James find a cougar shifter? Just how many shifters had they conned into this mission?

"I'm not going out there," the man across the clearing declared, gun up.

A hyena's yipping laugh sounded from nearby. I almost rolled my eyes. First off, there were no hyena shifters in this part of Wyoming. They were rare, and the only known families tended to hang out in Africa. Secondly, I recognized the call. My youngest brother, Andy, had been practicing the call for years. Something about high school girls getting a kick out of it. Whatever the reason for it, the sound was 100 percent effective at scaring the piss out of a couple of city soldiers who didn't know any better.

"What the fuck, man?" one cursed, jumping back a couple of feet.

Might not have been the most orthodox of plans, but it actually seemed to be working. Every time one of Conrad's gang got too close to the edge of the clearing, an animal growl or flash of amber eyes pushed them back. If only the law enforcement people would show up soon, we'd be good.

Nothing was that easy, though.

"I know you're out there, Mr. Granger." Conrad called.

Seriously, where were the law enforcement folk? I shot a look at William, hoping he could read my expression since speaking at this point was probably a bad idea. He was too busy watching the scene in front of us to notice my silent question. I reached over and pinched his hip. He managed to meet my eyes without moving his body or even his head. I widened my eyes and arched my brows. Either he'd pick up on the question, or he'd think I was having some kind of seizure. His shoulder moved infinitesimally in a shrug. Which was both good and bad. Good that he didn't think I'd completely lost my marbles. Bad that he didn't know where the good guys were either.

"I'm getting tired of these games." Conrad gestured to Mafia Hit Man, who followed at his heels like a faithful dog.

Mafia Hit Man nodded and made a gesture to Balding Blond Guy, who'd stayed in place near the SUV Conrad had gotten out of. A faithful guard dog.

Balding Blond Guy opened the hatchback of the SUV and dragged out something bulky and heavy. No, not some*thing*. Some*one*. He hauled out a man who'd been bound, hands and wrists, with silver duct tape and gagged with a red bandana.

I gasped, earning a warning look from James. Easy for him to be reactionless; he probably didn't recognize Jesse. But I did.

I hadn't seen him in person for a couple of years, not since we'd broken up, but there was no doubt it was him. The Marriott badge on his lapel confirmed it. The terror in his eyes made me want to look away. Guilt stopped me. If anything happened to Jesse, it would be my fault.

A rumbling growl from the other side of the clearing echoed through the air. It was the first time I'd heard Buddy. I'd almost forgotten he was supposed to be there, what with the plethora of my relatives, the wolves, and the mysterious cougar showing up to the party too.

Mafia Hit Man licked his lips nervously, and his gun came up. "Was that a bear?"

"Don't be stupid," Conrad snapped, but his hand edged closer to his belt as though reaching for a gun. "I understand this man is a friend of yours. You shouldn't have let him get involved in this mess."

Balding Blond Guy pulled a knife out of a sheath at his hip. Sunlight glinted off the sharp edge of the blade. My bowels turned to water as that razor's edge pressed against Jesse's throat.

Jesse gurgled something from behind the gag, his eyes rolling like a panicked horse. I'd probably be panicked too.

"I'll count to three."

At any other time, I would have scoffed at some international weapons trafficker using the old "count to three" mom trick, but today I took it for the promise it was.

I braced my hands to push myself up, but William's hand curled around my upper arm in an iron-hard grip I knew was going to leave a bruise.

"One."

I tugged at his hold, glaring at William, yelling at him silently to let me go. He ignored me.

"Two."

"Please," I whispered.

A tiny back-and-forth shake of his head. I could see the tearing indecision in his eyes. He didn't want anyone to be hurt either, but I guessed he was more worried about me. While I appreciated the sentiment, I refused to let Jesse be sacrificed. Not for me and my stupid plan.

I mouthed the word *sorry* to William. "Stop! I'm here!"

William let go of me, probably in shock, and I leaped to my feet. I waved behind me, gesturing for my brother to go, to run. I couldn't afford to turn around and make sure he obeyed.

"Let Jesse go. It's me you want." I stepped forward.

I felt more than saw the massive bulk that was William appear next to me. "No," he said. "I've had enough. Leave Donnie alone, release him and this man"—he gestured to Jesse—"and I'll cooperate."

I whirled on him. "What? No!"

"This ends now." William tossed his assault rifle onto the ground in front of him. The handguns and the knife quickly joined it.

I gaped, horrified, terrified. This couldn't be happening. "No, no, no…."

Conrad tipped his head toward us. "Kill them. All of them."

YOU know that slo-mo thing that happens in movies when shit is about to get real? Well, true story. I swear, time practically stopped.

Mafia Hit Man aimed his gun at me.

Balding Blond Guy tightened the grip on his knife.

Behind me, James loaded a shell into Dad's shotgun.

And me? I stood there like a statue watching everything unfold around me.

Then, as suddenly as time stopped, it sped forward at a hundred times regular speed. A massive grizzly bear, thick with prehibernation fat and winter fur, charged past the men on the east side of the clearing. Shouting and gunshots shook the air. Or maybe it was the thunder and lightning that exploded from above, heralding a bird with a twenty-foot wingspan, glossy black feathers, and wicked talons. Conrad's men didn't know what to do, where to aim. Some shot wildly into the air; others aimed at the massive bear.

At my side, James shifted into coyote form and yipped. Next thing I knew, a dozen coyotes and as many wolves rushed the clearing, growling and yipping.

The golden eagles who had played lookout, one owl, and a murder of crows darkened the sky, screeching, hooting, and cawing to wake the dead.

Buddy—the gigantic grizzly bear—bellowed, Jesse squeaked and fainted, and Balding Blond Guy dropped his dead weight. He reached for his gun, but before his fingers touched the handle, Buddy swiped at him with a paw the size of an iPad, throwing him against the SUV with a crunch. Though he still breathed, Balding Blond Guy didn't get up.

Buddy stood over Jesse's inert form and hollered a warning to anyone who got at all close.

Lightning flashed, hitting a winter-bare tree, sending sparks and smoke into the air. The electrical charge from the strike made two of Conrad's men shudder in place like bacon on a griddle. They fell to their knees, dazed.

Sometimes I really loved my roommate.

A coyote's pained yip pulled me from my stupid mannequin routine. *Andy.* I found my youngest brother limping into the woods, a bloody furrow along his flank. Before I could rush to him, James burst from a nearby thicket, crashing into the bastard who'd shot our brother. The man with the gun aimed his weapon at James. Before I had time to think about it, I snatched up the discarded rifle. My fingers fumbled over the safety even as I sprinted to my brother's aid. I tried twice more to release the safety before giving up and gripping the rifle like a baseball bat. I hauled the gun back and swung with all my strength, the stock making a sharp cracking noise at the contact with the stranger's head. The bastard gunman fell back, unconscious but alive.

Where the hell were the law enforcement people? How much longer was I going to have to stand around watching my family and friends get shot at?

Conrad and William still stood facing each other, silent pillars among chaos. Neither reacted when a cougar bounded after a black-attired bad guy, or when a crow dive-bombed another shooter, causing his shot to go wide.

"Why are you doing this?" William asked. "You were better than this, better than your father." He stepped forward.

Why was William chatting with this dude? Was he hoping for some grand confession? No, I realized after a moment's thought. He wasn't angling for a confession— he was trying to keep Conrad distracted.

Hatred blazed in Conrad's gaze. He wanted William dead. Whatever his reasons, they were significant and personal.

"This isn't what you want, Robert." William used his professor voice, the calm, controlled voice that sometimes made me feel protected and sometimes make me want to slap him. Conrad must have had a similar reaction.

"You have no idea what I want." Conrad's French accent thickened with emotion. "You were like family, and you betrayed that family. You betrayed the man who looked upon you as a son."

Yep. It was personal all right.

"And for what? A job? Money? You betrayed his trust—my trust—for a job."

William didn't say anything. On the other hand, what could he say? I doubted there was any excuse or platitude William could give that would lessen the grief or anger or whatever it was Conrad felt. It had been a job. And revenge. But William wasn't likely to share that part of his motivation.

"Donnie."

What with the growls, shrieks, gunshots, and everything, something as simple as William saying my name almost didn't register.

"Get the keys out of the SUVs."

Oh, right. I looked around. Conrad's men, including Mafia Hit Man, were being herded toward the center of the clearing, just as I'd hoped. Of course, it wouldn't take much for one of them to start the car and drive out, no matter how many crows dive-bombed them.

I dashed to the first SUV, grateful the vehicle used an actual key. I had a nanosecond to worry that these SUVs were new enough to only need fobs in proximity instead of an actual key.

A terrible taste settled on the back of my tongue, like scales on dead leaves. It was a scent but so much more, and it clued me in that there was more trouble to be had than the bad guys filling the clearing. I searched the surrounding bushes and trees, desperate to find the source of that odor. There was something purely evil about it. Twice my eyes skimmed past the barely twitching brown leaf on a mostly bare bush before I saw it. Her.

That Vasquez chick—the one who was apparently aces when it came to torturing information out of people—lay mostly submerged in a pile of dead leaves, the tip of one wicked-ass gun barely visible. If the movies and television shows I'd watched in the past were the least bit accurate, that gun was a sniper rifle, and it was pointing straight at William's back.

I reacted without thought. I raced to William, hurdling a couple of Conrad's men who lay unconscious in my way. I screamed something—maybe the word "no" or "stop" or maybe it was a wordless bellow.

My sharp coyote vision focused on Vasquez's finger as it squeezed. For every micrometer the trigger moved, my heart pounded even faster. I wasn't fast enough. No one was fast enough to beat a sniper's bullet, but that didn't stop me from trying.

The concussive *boom* shattered the still air almost before the gun fired.

I launched myself the remaining distance between William and me, but I was too late.

The force of the bullet spun William around, and blood splattered into the air.

I'd created enough momentum with my leap that when my body collided with his, William and I crashed onto the ground in a tangled heap.

"Oh God, William!"

His face was milk pale, his jaw clenched against the pain.

"Please be all right. Please be all right." I found the growing wetness on his chest and couldn't catch my breath. The thick liquid didn't show red on the black fabric, but there was no doubt in my mind that it was William's blood soaking through.

I tore at his shirt, ripping it from bottom hem to throat. Then I saw the crimson stain and had to fight the silver flecks of unconsciousness that tried to overwhelm me.

So much blood. This was all my fault.

I pulled off my dark gray hoodie and tried to wipe away the blood enough to see the extent of the wound.

"Donnie." My name sounded far away, echoing and faint.

I finally found the source of the blood, an angry hole about the size of a nickel. I pressed the thick cloth of my hoodie against the wound. High on the chest, inches above and to the left of the heart. Practically the shoulder.

"Donnie."

I didn't want to see the damage to his back.

This was wrong. William wasn't supposed to get hurt.

"Donnie."

Finally my name penetrated. Probably because it was being said with William's mouth. I pulled my gaze away from the bloody hole in his chest to look into his face. "William?" He was still pale, and pain tightened his lips, but he was completely aware. "You're not dead!"

"That's the second time you've told me that," he said, covering my hand with his where it lay pressed to his chest. "You've gotta stop worrying."

"Sure," I agreed, not even aware of what I agreed to. He wasn't dead, and it seemed he wasn't dying. Everything else could be worked out. Later.

Suddenly the silence surrounding us registered. The sound of birds, animal growls, howls, yips, and gunshots was missing. A waiting tension filled the air instead.

I looked over my shoulder.

All of Conrad's men sat on the ground, legs folded in front of them. A ring of coyotes and wolves surrounded them. Twenty feet away, a pile of guns and knives of every shape and size sat under the watchful gaze of a cougar, who I now recognized as one of James's best friends. Gary something.

Conrad lay facedown a little ways away with a massive grizzly bear paw pressed into his back. Buddy's lips undulated with the constant warning growls emanating from his throat.

Vasquez wasn't among them.

James had shifted back to human form, as had Ford. I don't know where Ford had stashed his clothes, because they wouldn't have survived his stint as a thunderbird, and he was quite clearly dressed. Both men had guns pointing at Conrad's men.

The shocked expressions on Conrad's men would have been hysterical if William hadn't been bleeding out in front of me. Several of the guys kept muttering "wolves" and "bears" and looking around as though in a dream.

An owl hooted nine times—three slow, three fast, three slow—a bird's version of SOS. I suppose Morse code was as good a communication tool as any.

I jerked my head up, looking for Ford. If more of Conrad's men were on their way, we were screwed.

Ford shook his head. "The cavalry."

Then I heard sirens in the distance.

It was about fucking time.

Chapter Eighteen

SIXTY-SEVEN days, six hours, and some-odd minutes had passed since the fight in the clearing. It had been sixty-seven days, five hours, and some-odd minutes since I last spoke with William. During that time, a bunch of stuff changed. My relationship with my family was better. They stopped pressuring me to work in the oil fields, no matter how much better the pay was compared to Buddy's. Either because they accepted the fact that I was content where I was, or because I finally told them in no uncertain terms that if they didn't drop it, I'd leave, just as they feared all along. Strangely enough, it worked.

I still worked at Buddy's, but a lot had changed there too. Buddy made me the general manager. Clearly the man had lost his mind. No sane person would make me manager of anything. A week after the fight, he grumbled something about loyalty and leadership, then handed me a set of keys. When I asked about the scope of my newfound power, he grunted and told me to do whatever I wanted. So I did.

No more prefrozen, microwavable menu options. No more generic salads. Fresh-baked pastries and locally sourced sandwich ingredients filled the display cases. Sure, the prices went up a smidge to offset the increased food costs, but no one was complaining. In fact, the biggest criticism I got had to do with running out of a particular treat.

The promotion came with a raise, which was great, because I'd also enrolled in Cody College's culinary program for the spring semester. The extra pay would help offset the cost of part-time tuition. I had to do the part-time thing since the café already took up loads more time than it used to. The difference between manager and barista, I guessed.

"He's here again." Ford reached past me to grab a bear claw, one of the café's newest treats in honor of Buddy.

I very deliberately didn't look up. As if I hadn't noticed the second William crossed the threshold. Every day for the last eighteen days, consistent as sunrise, William came into Buddy's, ordered a plain black coffee, one of whichever pastries I was showcasing that day, and settled in at his usual table, where he sat for the next seventy-four minutes.

Every. Single. Day.

It was torture.

I tried *so hard* to let it go, to give him his space. The danger was done, the forced proximity was done, and so we were done. Done. Done. Done.

I'd hoped and prayed and wished I could get over him and move on. Just like I'd done with the other crushes in my life that didn't work out. Just like William had probably done. But I couldn't shake the need I had for him. At first I thought he was on board with the avoidance plan. He'd stayed away for almost two months—forty-nine days for anyone who was counting, which I certainly was not. Curiosity ate at me like acid, but I managed to avoid stopping by the social sciences building or planting myself in front of his town house. Every day that went by, the acid burned stronger, not easing in the least.

Then, after forty-nine days of absence, he walked into Buddy's like nothing had changed.

But so much had changed. Too much.

So, every time he walked in, I managed to find something to do in the office or the kitchen. I'd spend that hour and fourteen minutes of his visit calculating food costs and profit margins, supplier invoices and payroll, anything to keep me behind claustrophobia-inducing closed doors.

Today there was a crowd and I couldn't afford to desert Ford. Which meant I couldn't hide. Sometimes having to be a responsible adult sucked big-time.

I could feel William's eyes on me as he waited in line to order his coffee.

My hands shook as I tried to attach a lid to the cup of peppermint hot chocolate. Ford grabbed the cup from me before I dumped the scalding drink all over the floor.

After handing the hot chocolate to a coed wearing a ski hat, he stalked to the pot of coffee, dumped some in a cup, then slammed the cup down on the counter. "I've had enough of this." He glared at William with enough heat, I was surprised the coffee didn't boil out over the cup's rim.

William met his gaze, the mild-mannered professor in his face, though something in his dark eyes told me he wasn't as placid as he appeared.

"You two need to either hash this out or you"—he jabbed a finger at William—"need to get the hell out of here and don't come back." He pointed at me this time. "And you. I'm tired of your moping. Take a seat and work your shit out."

"But the customers—"

"Will have to wait their turn." Ford rolled his eyes. "Go."

I met William's eyes for the first time in over two months, and just like that, all the air was sucked out of the room and the other people faded away.

"Hey." My voice was thin, breathless. Not at all the confident, take-charge man I was trying to be.

"Can we talk?"

I tucked my hands into my pockets. "Why now?"

Someone cleared their throat. A customer trying to order. William's massive form blocked their access to Ford. He stepped aside, letting the middle-aged woman through. William cupped my elbow and urged me toward his usual table by the fire. The smoldering warmth of the flames had nothing on the heat of his hand on me. Even through the knit of my sweater, I could feel each point of contact, my skin practically singeing at the touch.

I mourned the loss of his hand on me the minute I sat. Stupid, traitorous body. He dropped his satchel next to the chair and shrugged out of a heavy brown jacket that was probably not the leather it appeared to be. I couldn't imagine William in real leather. Underneath, he wore a familiar oatmeal-colored sweater. The one that made me want to curl up into his lap and burrow into the soft wool. Was it a coincidence?

"You've been avoiding me."

"*Excuse me?*" That certainly hadn't been what I expected him to say. "I've been avoiding you? You're the one who disappeared for a month and a half." Forty-nine days. "Without a word."

"I was in Prague, without access to phone or email."

"Prague?"

He nodded. "After I got out of the hospital, I had to make a statement regarding the events in October."

I cringed. I really didn't need memories of his hospital visit. After the law enforcement people arrived and took Conrad and his men into custody, William had been rushed to the hospital in Cody. His agency folk must have had some serious pull, because as soon as we reached the medical center, William had been whisked away. No one would tell me what was going on. No one would let me talk with him. I planted myself in the waiting room and made a nuisance of myself until someone in a black suit carrying an official-looking badge came by and informed me that William had been taken elsewhere, and if I didn't want to find myself in jail, I'd better leave.

I asked where William was. I got no answer.

I asked them to have William call me. I didn't get any phone calls.

"You're a freaking secret agent. You couldn't find some way to let me know you were alive? For forty-nine days, I waited." I cringed. Damn it, now he knew I'd counted the days. I charged ahead anyway. Maybe he'd missed it. "I had no way to know if you were coming back, no way to know if anything happened to you."

"I didn't have a choice. There was the matter of identifying the traitors who gave up my identity to Conrad's men."

That stopped me. "Did you find them?"

He nodded.

"So you're safe now?"

He nodded again.

The relief I felt pissed me off. "I'm glad you're safe. But that doesn't change anything. You went radio silent for almost two months while I had no idea what was going on. And then you just show up like nothing happened? Just kept going on with your routine? Screw that."

I pushed my chair back to stand, but he stopped me with a hand on my wrist. "Before you leave, I have something for you." He grabbed his satchel from the ground by his feet. From it, he pulled out a plastic food-storage container. It looked like the one I'd given him the day I finally got up the nerve to approach William all those weeks ago. He set it on the table between us. "The scones were amazing, by the way."

"Yeah?" There was some kind of colored paper inside the container, the tissue kind used for Christmas presents. I reached out to touch the container, hesitated before my fingers could make contact.

"It won't bite."

At first I thought William was laughing at me, but then I realized it was nervousness I heard in his voice, not humor.

He scratched his beard absently; then, as if realizing he was doing it, he folded his hands on the table in front of him. For someone as controlled and deliberate as William, those small gestures were tantamount to someone wringing their hands. He cleared his throat. "I hoped to give this to you for Christmas. But, well, you were avoiding me."

Christmas had been two weeks ago. And, yeah, I'd been avoiding him.

I held my breath and popped open the top of the plastic container. Inside, the edges were layered with red tissue paper, and there were dozens of white paper slips. I plucked one folded strip out. It was a receipt from Buddy's. On it, someone with blocky, bold handwriting— presumably William—had written *March 3. First time I saw you. Your energy, your smile, hooked me.*

My fingers trembled as I smoothed the receipt out. I couldn't bring myself to look up. I pulled another strip of paper out. It was another Buddy's receipt. This one, written with blue ink, said *May 19. I hate finals week. I stopped by today just to see your smile. It helped. You always help.*

My heart pounded so hard in my chest, I thought the vibrations of it would bounce me out of my seat. I snatched a third piece of paper from the bucket. This one was from September. *Some guy kissed you today. It almost killed me to see it. But if he makes you happy, that is enough for me.* I had to think about that. When had someone kissed me at the café? September? Right. One of my exes had come back for a family thing and had stopped by. The kiss hadn't been passionate or anything. It had been quick, a "glad to see you" kind of kiss.

I very carefully smoothed out the receipt and set it with the other two. "Is this real? I mean, this isn't some kind of elaborate joke, right?"

In answer, William pulled out another stack of receipts from his jacket pocket. He held them out to me. Maybe I should have played it cool or done something to maintain some distance and dignity, but there was nothing in the world that was going to keep me from those slips of paper. I snatched them and started to read. There was one from each of the last eighteen days. Each one had the same message. *I love you.*

Dizziness swamped me, and my vision blurred. Everything around me was turning a sickly gray-green. I scooted the chair back and folded myself over until my head hung between my knees. In a second William was there, crouched in front of me, his broad, rough hand running up and down my spine in a soothing gesture.

"Breathe, Donnie."

I gasped and laughed at the same time, which sounded a bit like a dying walrus trying to sing. The light-headedness had passed, thankfully, but it took another few seconds before my voice came to me. "You know stalking's a crime, right?"

He grinned. I could have counted the number of times I'd seen him smile on one hand. The sight of his wide, happy grin made giddy warmth pool up inside me. "Takes a stalker to know a stalker," he said.

"Fair point." I braced my hands on my knees and pushed myself into a sitting position. "So, I think we need to talk. Somewhere private."

"My place?"

The idea was a little nerve-racking, but I didn't have a better suggestion. I would stay disciplined. I could keep my hands to myself and refrain from jumping him in the living room. Maybe. If I tried.

I stopped by the bustling counter on our way out. I clutched the food storage container full of receipts to my chest. There were dozens I had yet to read. Ford shot me a baleful glare. I ignored it. "Call Kelly, see if she can cover. I've got some stuff to work out."

"Figured." Ford grunted and shot whipped cream onto someone's latte. "I called her ten minutes ago. She's on her way."

"Oh. Well, good. I'll see you later."

"You owe me one," he muttered, grabbing the credit card from a customer. "Actually, you owe me a bunch."

"Yeah, yeah."

WILLIAM drove us to his town house in silence. I've always known he wasn't one for chatter, but we were going to have to work on his communication skills. In fact, that's the first thing I told him when we entered his home. "We need to work on your communication skills. Taciturn is one thing. Completely blocked off is another."

He led me to the couch. We sat on opposite ends, because if I cuddled in too close, we wouldn't get any of the talking done that we needed to do. I hoped he did it for the same reason.

"I don't think you're a child."

My mouth opened and closed a couple of times in surprise. That hadn't been where I expected the conversation to start. "Well, that's good. Because I'm not."

"I'm not good with words. Not when it comes to"—he waved his hand between us—"talking. Not when it's important."

"From what I saw, you're great with words. Not wordy, by any means, but you get your point across." I shook the container of receipts to illustrate my point. It made an odd clicking noise I hadn't heard before, like there was a quarter or something hard inside.

"Not when it comes to you. I spent the last ten years either learning to be or pretending to be someone—

something—I'm not. I couldn't afford to let my emotions show. So I kept them hidden. Sometimes they were hidden so well, I wasn't sure I even had emotions anymore."

I set the plastic container on the coffee table next to me and reached for William.

"I moved to Cody, ready to start the quiet, boring life I'd always wanted."

I raised my eyebrows at that. Who actually *wants* to live a quiet, boring life? Well, probably someone who'd spent the last several years hanging out with international weapons traffickers. But even at his placid, self-contained best, I knew there was more to William than quiet and boring.

"Then, when I was sure the monotony of it all was going to drive me insane, I walked into Buddy's for a cup of coffee."

My heartbeat picked up.

"You were so full of life, of energy, you made me feel alive. For the first time since Jasper died, I felt alive. But you are so young."

And there it was. I pulled my hand away.

William snatched it back. "Please. Just give me a chance. You are young—you're ten years younger than me, and you're sweet and idealistic in a way I've never been. I watched you for six months, convinced there was no chance in hell someone like you would be interested in someone like me."

I snorted. "You underestimate your appeal. I'd bet money that half the students in your classes get just as moony as I do. You've got this intensity about you. And you're solid. People feel safe around you." Now it was my turn to struggle with words. *Solid* and *safe* sounded like father figure rather than lover. "And then there's the fact that you're the sexiest man I've ever met. I wanted to climb you like Everest every day for months. And, William?"

He met my eyes.

"I wasn't exactly subtle about it. That's what started this whole mess, if you recall—people noticing my crush. You couldn't have missed that."

He shrugged. "I told myself I was seeing what I wanted to see, not what was really there."

"Then let me make it clear. I fell for you the minute you walked into Buddy's that first time. Then, as I got to know you, I fell harder and harder."

A slow smile spread across his face.

"Which is why, when I thought you were treating me like a kid or an idiot, it hurt so much."

He winced. "Yeah. Which brings me back to I don't think of you as a child. I was terrified, more afraid than I've ever been, that you'd be taken from me like Jasper had been. My need to control everything had nothing to do with lack of faith in you. I didn't trust anyone else to keep you safe. I focused on what I knew and the resources I had. I should have let you help, but I didn't want you to see me like that, in special ops mode. I don't like the man I was when I was undercover. I didn't ever want you to see me in that light."

And to think I thought he needed to work on communicating. If he kept that up, I'd be a sobbing puddle on his hardwood floors. "Okay. Okay. I get that. I do. But if you want us to be together, you're going to have to work on that. I love you for who you are. Each and every piece. Your past, your present, and your future." A sudden thought occurred. I slapped a hand to my jeans pocket, the one holding the eighteen newest notes. "You do want to be together, right?"

He reached for the plastic box of paper slips and pulled the lid off. After digging in a minute, he pulled out an old-fashioned gift tag, complete with a twine loop, on which hung a shiny silver house key.

I took it from him. Writing on the tag, in the now-familiar thick, bold block letters, said *Move in with me?*

I clenched the key in my fist and pressed it to my heart. And I squeaked. Yeah, squeaked. *Use your words, Donnie.* "Ah… *yes.*" I licked my lips. "I mean yes, yes I'll live with you. If you're sure."

William grinned again, making me need fingers from both hands to count the number of smiles I'd seen from him. He hauled me across the couch and plopped me on his lap.

I laughed. "Have I mentioned how much I love it when you get all aggressive on me?"

He pressed his mouth to mine, trapping my bottom lip between his teeth. He released the hold, then licked the spot softly, soothingly. "Yeah? I might have to change one of my plans, then."

I wrapped my arms around his neck and stared into those dark, dark eyes. "What plan?"

He bent his head to nuzzle at that spot where shoulder and neck meet, the spot that had me squirming. "Yeah. In six months I was going to ask you to marry me. But if you like aggressive, maybe I'll just order you to marry me."

At that completely unexpected announcement, I jerked back so violently I almost fell off my perch on his lap. Only his strong hands at my waist kept me from ending up in a heap at his feet.

"What… you… six months?" I croaked, my brain seizing, the words jumbling on my tongue. "Why six months?"

"Give us time to make sure we can live together without killing each other, for one. And give us time to find a better house. You'll want one with a bigger kitchen than what I have here at the town house. It will be summer then, and we'll have a break from school to plan everything."

If this had been a cartoon, I'm pretty sure my eyes would have sprung out of their sockets, heart-shaped and glowing red. "I love you."

He cupped my face. "I love you too."

I couldn't contain the sheer joy exploding inside me. I wrapped my arms around his neck and my legs around his torso and squeezed him in a full-body hug.

I snuggled into him, practically trying to merge completely in him, to surround myself with that scent that was entirely William. We stayed like that for a while, me absently touching him, him squeezing me tight as though he couldn't stomach letting me go, not even for a second. It was like we were making up for those miserable sixty-seven days we'd been apart. Best of all, there were no crazy weapons traffickers after us and no humans threatening me with phallic produce. We had peace. It was about the best thing I could imagine.

Things weren't going to be perfect forever—our personalities were too opposite for us not to butt heads occasionally—but that was kind of perfect too. Every life needed a little drama now and then. Besides, we were perfect for each other. I needed a little dependable, solid, and safe in my life to offset my periodically distracted, more-often-than-not hyperactive personality. And he needed someone to keep him from taking himself too seriously, someone to remind him to have fun. And I was just the coyote for the job.

I stretched a bit so I could brush my mouth against his. He let loose a contented rumble that I felt in his chest more than heard. I grinned into the kiss, and he ran his hand down the length of my spine. Yeah, this was pretty much perfect. I could picture us together like this for the rest of our lives.

I loved him and he loved me. And we were getting married. We'd see about that six months crap, though. I bet I'd be able to talk him into proposing in three months, tops. We were going to need every week of the summer break between semesters for the wedding and honeymoon.

Coming in October 2017

⟲REAMSPUN BEYOND

Dreamspun Beyond #5
Dragon's Hoard by M.A. Church

To be loved by a dragon is to be treasured.

A hundred years ago, werewolf Alpha Montgomery took a risk driven by desperation—he borrowed money from the ancient dragon Warwick Ehecatl, putting up the pack lands as collateral. Now the debt is due, and dragons don't forget—or forgive. Warwick demands Montgomery's son, Avery, and three businesses as compensation. As an Omega, Avery knows he is basically useless to his pack, so he might as well agree. He soon has second thoughts, though. Warwick is fearsome, and he's free to do as he likes with Avery.

Warwick knows his race's reputation, and he even admits some of it is deserved. But he'd rather cut off his tail than let his innocent mate's light go out. It won't be easy, but buried deep, there's something between them worth safeguarding.

Dreamspun Beyond #6
The Supers by Sean Michael

Hunting ghosts and finding more than they bargained for.

Blaine Franks is a member of the paranormal research group the Supernatural Explorers. When the group loses their techie to a cross-country move, newly graduated Flynn Huntington gets the job. Flynn fits in with the guys right off the bat, but when it comes to him and Blaine, it's more than just getting along.

Things heat up between Blaine and Flynn as they explore their first haunted building, an abandoned hospital, together. Their relationship isn't all that progresses, though, and soon it seems that an odd bite on Blaine's neck has become much more.

Hitchhiking ghosts, a tragic love story forgotten by time, and the mystery of room 204 round out a romance where the things that go bump in the night are real.